Adnan Mahmutović is a Bosnian- ... and lecturer in English literature. He became a refugee of war in 1993 and has since written on the myths of home.

Also by Adnan Mahmutović

NOVEL:
Thinner than a Hair

LITERARY CRITICISM:
Ways of Being Free

Adnan Mahmutović

How to Fare Well and Stay Fair

SALT

CROMER

PUBLISHED BY SALT PUBLISHING

12 Norwich Road, Cromer NR27 0AX United Kingdom

© Adnan Mahmutović, 2012

The right of Adnan Mahmutović to be identified as the author of this work has been asserted by him in accordance with Section 77 of the Copyright, Designs and Patents Act 1988.

Salt Publishing 2012

Printed in Great Britain by the MPG Books Group, Bodmin and King's Lynn

Typeset in Paperback 9 / 10

ISBN 978 1 907773 28 0 paperback

1 3 5 7 9 8 6 4 2

The weight of this sad time we must obey,
Speak what we feel, not what we ought to say.

—Shakespeare, *King Lear*

CONTENTS

How to Fare Well and Stay Fair

HOW TO FARE WELL
AND STAY FAIR

1993–2012

i.

Cry when you leave your country, if you absolutely must. If you're an expat, please, don't even think about it, but if you're a refugee, make sure you do it out of sight of other cry-babies. You do not want to encourage them, or speed up the progress of their bouts of nostalgia, and feed all the weird bugs they've been infected with from the moment they were packed on those old blue buses, which used to take you to school and your father to his factory job, but which are now used to take you so far north that red-nosed Rudolf has to hide from your sorry face behind frozen trees.

ii.

Don't sit in the aisle, even though there are no seats left for all the guys and girls of your age. You're young and healthy and not yet smart enough to understand the war and what could have happened to you, and this is why you will one day say that those warm war days were the happiest moments of your life, when soldiers roamed about and shot at will and you spent hours sitting tight with Mother and Father in your neighbour's cellar, because it was less damp and less infested with rats than yours. On the bus, you can sit with half your arse on an armrest, because the girl in the seat will not tell you to fuck off and she may smile and you may like her buck teeth and the weird perm and the Tintin tuft, and even though you will not see her again after this long ride, you will remember that she did not tell you to sit on the fucking floor from where you couldn't look down her blouse but only at her sandals and black nail polish.

iii.

When you arrive at Świnoujście, the sight of the Baltic waters will make you want to urinate, I mean piss, so go to the left towards the skinny old Polish woman in rubber boots and no teeth to speak of. Do not look into the bucket between her legs when you go for the green door with the sign of a fat boy peeing into a pot through which someone has drilled a hole, for air circulation, you guess. Suck in your stomach, unless a year of war has already made you camp-skinny, relieve yourself, and if you cannot find the toilet paper — because you are not looking up at the little window high up above your head — just pull up your pants, and once you're out again you will see the woman is muttering stuff, and you WILL understand that she's cursing your guts, even though the only foreign language you've given a shot was German and you suck at German as much as at your motherfather tongue, and you will reach into your pocket for money. Please, pay for nr.2 even if you only did nr.1.

IV.

In the big refugee hangar in Ystad, the home of Kurt Wallander, after the quick interrogation in which you were asked if you had any money and you lied about the three hundred Deutsch Marks you've stashed in your shoe and which the soldiers on the border to Hungary had not found, do not take a shower and do not shave. It'll only make you restless and you won't be able to sleep and you'll spend the night listening to two hundred refugees breaking wind and snoring and, yes, crying.

V.

On the way to one of the refugee camps you will mispronounce names of all towns and villages on the motorway signs. When you arrive at Uddevalla, on the West Coast, the old sand-coloured military buildings will look like something from Dickens, and the ceilings will be three meters high, and the joint bathrooms big and airy, and you will share the room with another family of four, and in the middle of the room there will be a border made of lockers without locks, one side of the room for your family and the other for another set of strangers, but the beds will be soft enough even for all the pea-hating princesses. The other family has two small children, even though the woman is as old and shrivelled as her man's moustache is grey and long.

vi.

Stay away from everyone for your mental health's sake, and I cannot stress this enough, STAY AWAY, even if that will make you a reclusive weirdo which no girl, or boy, will even smirk at. The people in the camp may be speaking the so-called motherfather tongue, but they will be strangers, and no matter how many pop and rock songs they may know by heart, songs you like, they will not be familiar with the golden nuggets of comics, American or European, on which you were weaned more than your mother's milk. They will not know that Moebius and Jean Giraud are the same man, that is, before and after his use of magic mushrooms, and they won't even know that Enki Bilal is really the French version of Enes Bilalović. Some may know of Conan, but you won't give a damn. And stay away from the refugee girls. They too are trying to stay away from refugees, at least the fresh ones. And, of course, keep away from refugee boys. They're so full of the stuff that can only be cured by sex and they will not be getting any for any foreseeable future, and if you're a girl and you give in for whatever reason, they will ruin your reputation and you'll have that hanging around your neck during all the frequent transfers to other camps, which reminds me, you will be moved around the country a lot, and you will keep mispronouncing those names of places over and over. The transfers will give you a sense of change, of progress. Do not be fooled. Nothing will change. It's all a mind trick. But if it does work on you, well, good for you, ignorance is bliss.

vii.

Actually, two things will change. 1: Your parents' nostalgia will evolve, beyond any of Darwin's predictions, an unprecedented mutation like in *X-Men*, except it won't make them look cool, and they will not wear spandex, or anything that's not at least two sizes too big. Some will still love those disgusting colourful rustling sweat suits. 2: There will be bullies, also mutated, and unrivalled by anything even the imagination of Stan Lee was able to produce at the top of his game.

viii.

On the day when wintertime kicks in, you forget to set the clock right, and you wake up an hour too early and wait in the cold outside the canteen. After breakfast, there will be an outbreak of paranoia in the camp. Down at the gates, in the red house with billiards and table tennis, neither of which you're good at, you'll stand in a corner, watch the brag-boys play and laugh, and you may be sipping on a light beer, when the guys you secretly call Short-Story and Tall-Tale, or even Laurel and Hardy, will barge in yelling and dragging a man, neither your generation nor that of your parents, and they will push him against the wall and say, Take off your fucking pants! You will not understand what they're after until they shout, Show us your dick, you fucking asshole! And the man will cry back, I am circumcised. You may not understand it fully even then because the scene will be cut when the camp manager comes in and stops them from pulling down the man's pants. You will remain in the corner, watching them go away and the billiard-players will resume their game as if the big drama was only a draught and someone just needed to close the door. The mouse-like guy may say, Fucking Hell, and strike the ball so hard it will bounce off the black ball and fall onto the floor and roll under the hard sofa. You'll walk the empty yard up to your room, and say Hi to the old couple who are drinking coffee with your parents, and then you'll lie down on the bed closest to the window and furthest from the tall locker. The old people will talk about the news that war criminals have been detected in some of the refugee camps, the Serbs that are pretending to be refugees to escape from the forthcoming repercussions. Then you will understand why those boys were chasing that man, but you will wonder if that could be true, even though the man had a Serbian name, but then, as with many, he was a product of a mixed marriage. Fuck it, you'll say out loud and your father will ask, What was that? And you'll say, Nothing, Dad. Nothing at all.

ix.

One morning, a month after you've transferred to another camp, your mother will go out to get mail, dressed in her pink nightgown and your father's jacket and shoes, and you will think her hair has been awful and messy since you came to Sweden, and her hair was never like that when she worked in the shopping mall in your hometown. In the already-open mailbox, on which your surname was misspelled even after your complaint, she will find a thin sheet of paper, folded in the middle and taped, drenched in elk saliva. She will come in, in tears of course, and throw it on the kitchen table where you and your curly-haired brother are eating hot dogs for breakfast, and she will lay a kitchen cloth over it until it's dry and you will nibble at that hot dog as she opens this latest Red Cross message from her brother, after three months of silence, and the handsome handwriting will be crossed out with black marker pen and you will put down your hot dog and take it from her and try to figure out what it was that was so dangerous and political in the letter that required censure, but you won't be able to figure it out and your mother will move her eyes over it, back and forth, as if erasing the black palimpsest, hoping her brother will reappear.

x.

When the refugee manager sends you on your first job, cleaning the stables at a local farm, do not be too excited, it's something of a community service for which you will not get paid because you're already on the refugee-dole, or whatever you call that monthly aid. You won't get to ride any of the horses, and you'll stay for three months, after which you'll move to another job, a construction site, and your neighbour from the camp will go to your old place. Your neighbour will be excited to replace you, thinking he will be the one to get the permanent position, but after those three months he will come to the construction site and you will move on to sell second-hand stuff, and so on, the circle of life. Once you've tried every job in that tiny town, and everyone you know has tried everything, two years have passed, and you may think you'll get a job, and use all those new words you've learnt, save for the curses, but the boss will say, Your Swedish is not good enough. And you may want to say, But it's been good enough these three months. Do not give in to temptation.

xi.

Once you get a job, a real one, please, be thankful, but whatever you do, do not follow your Swedish colleagues' examples and complain all the time, even though you may be working double shifts, because they will tell you that you should be so lucky to have a job now that all the immigrants are stealing jobs from honest Swedish people, as well as their girls. Pretend that the second part is true even though no Swedish girl has even looked at you so far, and the one you fancy at work might just start doubting you're a dork and might think you're a player, and instead of a bargepole, she may touch you with all manner of other things. Don't forget to thank God if she does.

xii.

You may be the only refugee teenager in the village, and that may seem an incurable virus at the time, but don't take it easy with all the kids and their parents who laugh every single time they meet as if they haven't seen each other for a decade. You won't believe their sincerity, but let them have their way. And if they keep telling each other what amazing and rich lives they used to have and how much they long to go home, resist saying any of the following: Why in the world are you so cheerful now? Why the hell don't you go back? Why have you started mixing languages already?

xiii.

Take classes in painting, photography, textile design and ceramics in Mullsjö Folkhögskola, which lies on the other side of the town five miles from your flat, and which you will love in wintertime because you will lose so much weight trudging through the waist-high snow. Forget about the textiles. The teacher may be a cosy old Swede, but she will remind you too much of your mother. You will abandon painting portraits and making sculptures because of your misinterpretation of the sacred text and because the French teacher will tell you in an accent worse than yours that you paint like a god, but eventually you will excel in pottery and photography. Do not bother buying that old Leica. It'll suck. The school has a nice old Hasselblad, not the one used on the first trip to the moon, but it'll be perfect to photograph the moon from the evergreen woods. It's big, the moon, and sometimes you will see twin moons, two crescents, not because you're going loony but because you've read too much Corto Maltese and you're an incorrigible romantic, whatever you may say to other people.

xiv.

Bring your father with you deep into the woods, where you found an old frozen cabin, snow up to the windows, cracked and dirty, the walls made of wooden tile-like pieces, lain in rows like fish scales, only rough and dark red and perfect as a background for refugee portraits. Ask your father to stand against it and start shooting. You will like the fact that you have to hunch over the Hasselblad because the window is on the top. It'll make you aware of where you stand and how you stand in relation to the object, and it'll make it hard to take a picture. Hasselblad does not allow for snapshots. Sabur. Patience. Your father will smile. Tell him, Stop smiling for God's sake. Look like a miserable refugee. He won't stop. He'll laugh and smirk and guffaw and chortle and do any other take on cheerfulness, and the borrowed Hasselblad will capture that, the true, the good, the spiteful. Years later you will frame that photo and remember that your father was the only one in the entire community who said, I do not long to go back. I have everything I need right here. At the time you will have given him a hard time because he doesn't conform and because everyone thinks he has no feelings, no sense of home and belonging. If you meet any of those people, years after you all become integrated and naturalised, don't bother saying Hi to them, even though they will smile their big smiles and look like they've missed you so much.

xv.

Go to Stockholm to visit your childhood friend. When you arrive at the Central Station two hours too early, with a map you cannot read and PO Box address only, do not try and walk all the way to the Liljeholmen refugee camp. The distance is at least ten times greater than you imagined. Just go back to the platform and wait for your friend to come, skinny and tall, and wearing an oversize jacket, black of course, and he will hug you and lift you off the ground and holler something into your ear and he will lead you down into the T-bana where small blue trains swish in every direction and there, after you bump into strangers, your friend will call you a village boy and teach you a few unwritten rules about proper conduct. For four days you will see Stockholm through a haze, and once you return to it you will not recognize it. On your second visit you'll meet another childhood friend and discover that he has a sister you've never met, even though their house was two miles from your house, and for the following two years you will hunt cheap bus tickets to come over and see her, and you'll spend all your refugee aid on the phone calls and letters stuffed with roses you plucked from the public garden, even though you were told it was illegal. She'll tell you they were still fresh and fragrant when they arrived three days later and you will believe her.

xvi.

When you depart for Stockholm from Jönköping bus station, as a farewell, your mother will call you names, such as traitor, and your father will cry silently and tell her you're a big boy now and you'll do well, or fare well, on your own, but she will treat you like a traitor for a few more years, even when you get married and give her a grandson, and she may look happy but she will cry because you are far away from her and too close to your in-laws as if you weren't man enough and she married you off, as if she had to pay your dowry rather than get one. Actually, there would be no dowry.

xvii.

Stockholm. Now that's a place to be lost in, especially at night, preferably Monday to Thursday, when there are no drunks that holler things you don't understand while you're walking to the bakery that opens its back door around 3am, and the bakers go out to smoke and they may give you warm buns every time, talk about things of substance, like flour and yeast and water, and maybe even butter. Medborgar-platsen, the citizen-square, will be the one where you will return time and again, and walk from the chocolate factory in the East, through the alley with a theatre in the cellar of a light-grey building, by the Tar-café, and take a right by the brick building, Katarina Norra Folkskola, which may look like a smaller royal quarters but was built a century earlier for some 1,400 pupils. In the modern schoolyard kids will be doing kids' stuff, and you will wish you were young enough to go to that school because the one in your hometown looked like the factory where your father worked, except for the orchard, yes, the orchard was the place to hide from girls and the football freaks and the basketball freaks and all other sports fans. Turn left and walk straight through the church-yard of Katarinakyrkan, with graves old enough to have the professions of the dead beneath the names, and a few new stones with mere names, and small black lanterns and fresh wreaths around them. You will like that no gravestone is like any other, and you may never go into that bright-coloured church with black roofs and golden clock-hands, which makes the graves look puny, but you will sit on the short grass between the graves, or you will lie on the green benches and read books and fall asleep and be nudged by beggars and you may sleepwalk away from them before you realise you should have given them the sandwich you haven't eaten or the Mars bar, and look up at the church again thinking what's the most hackneyed word you could use for it, maybe majestic, yes, it does look majestic standing erect like that above the graves. Walk down the one-way street, pass the old house with a small attic window which will remind you of your attic in Banja Luka, and you will imagine, somehow, magically living there and writing the masterpiece worthy of Strindberg, but the dream will end with the short street when you exit between the cheese shop and the bookstore-barbershop, both with black windows, and for a few years you will pass an old fire station, but after the turn of the century, that will be a mosque, and you will think how amazingly appropriate that the architect kept the flair of the place, except for the ugly minaret, short with a top that looks like a witch's hat, nothing like the tall and slender Turkish-style minarets in your hometown. You will get a call from work. Yes, you will have work now. You got it in 1998, even though you were late for the interview with the wheelchaired man whose carer you'd become and with whom you'd stay for eleven years and whose smile would be the beginning of a beautiful friendship, no irony intended. Your boss will tell you the Finnish woman who was supposed to work the night shift has come down with stomach flu, and you will think how this excuse always works if you want to skip work, but you will never use it. You will look over the red and black and green rooftops of south Stockholm and say, for the first time, I'm sorry, but I'm not in town. I'm in Jönköping visiting my parents. I'd love to pitch in and help you guys out, but I don't think I can make it.

xviii.

Not long after that sunny day of mosque opening, when you walk the same path with your wife pushing a baby carriage, and eat the cheap kebab with no onions and bitter lettuce but with extra red sauce, the planes will crash into the

WTC, but you won't find out about it until you come to work, and the carer who worked the day shift will be laughing and you won't believe that thing was anything but a Hollywood movie, not until, a few days later, you will fear going to the mosque. You will look suspiciously at the strangers you actually liked meeting every Friday noon for the jumah prayer, and they might look suspiciously at each other, and at you, or maybe not at you because you're too white, as many will tell you, you're a white Muslim, and you won't be singled out at airports, even though your name may stand out from your Swedish passport, and you will tell them that you have never gone by plane, ever, anywhere, and that you don't expect to because you can't afford it.

xix.

Two more children and a Ph.D later, the police officer, whom you call the Guardian of the Mosque, will still say Hi every time he sees you, even though you will never introduce yourself or find out his name. He'll give a smile to all the worshippers that stream in and out of the mosque, even in cold winds when he keeps blowing into his cupped hands, and he'll smile even at those few smokers who always gather around him. If you have a baby carriage with you, or stuff, like big bags, which you don't want to bring inside, leave them there, he won't mind, he won't check them for dangerous substances. You will find them untouched. Put your baby in the carriage and walk around the building. It'll take longer to get to the citizen square than to go down the 101 stairs you used to take, but that'd be too tough on your back. You're no longer twenty. Face it.

xx.

After the prayer, take the bus, or even better, walk down Götgatan, then turn left before you get to Victoria, the old cinema where they have just opened a Fairtrade coffee shop called Barista, and walk all the way to Skanstull Church, then cut through the old park and go all the way to the waterfront, and then follow the cobbled street and take the ferry home. Do not read on the ferry, as you always do, or listen to audio books. Just watch the water and the tame wild-ducks, and the wild wild-swans and the black weird-birds. Back home, you will have a pile of essays to grade, a story to tweak, emails to answer, but your wife will be home with your sick daughter and the boys will want to tell you about the latest fight they got into, so make two cups of coffee and camomile tea, take them all out to the balcony, and procrastinate.

[REFUGE]E

Home. I pull my forehead from the lukewarm bus window with this word bouncing inside my head. My name is Almasa, but I'm an anonymous woman on a bus full of Bosnians heading for the Swedish west coast, to Uddevalla refugee camp. It is December 1993. I'm . . . eighteen . . . I think. Even though the bus is full, no one sits next to me, not even any of the ugly teenagers, not since the tall one touched my hair and asked me to join them in the front of the bus where they sang pop songs about booze and sex on the beach, and I said, Go back and tell your pals I'll bite off your little dicks if you don't stop singing. He did. I expected more resistance from our youth.

Ho?me, I write on the window, inscribing a question mark in the word's core. As if tasting unfamiliar food, I move my thin, pale lips, whispering, 'Ho?me, no place like it.' I want to be consumed in longing, in tear-shedding, heart-aching, mind-burning longing for my motherland. I don't. Crossing borders does not make me homesick. Not even crossing a line of no-turning-back, back to where I should belong by the rule of birth. I want to break the warm window and thrust a shard in my thigh, just to see if my body will thrash in pain. I fail to be a normal refugee.

Outside, the wind is running a hurdle race over clouds and the evergreen Swedish forests look like the countries I passed through on my way out of the Balkan war, the countryside like the scrambled eggs with spinach that Mum used to make on Sundays, to make us stronger, of course. I love this bitter -smelling Swedish bus, with its clean black and grey seats big enough to shield me from the passengers in front of me, and the ceiling with soft lights for those who like reading, and air conditioning for those who like to be cooled, even in winter.

In June 1993, the old Bosnian bus on the way north to any country that would have us, was smouldering in the early summer heat. People sat in the aisle, children jumped on the torn seats, their movements sending up wafts of dust. It was like a bus from exotic films, with luggage and bigger animals on the roof and smaller poultry flying back and forth inside. Bus sweet bus. Ho?me sweet ho?me. I tried to draw a face on the dirty window without lifting my finger from the glass. The bus bobbed up and the figure's hair turned wavy just like mine. I whispered, 'Hi Dad. Nice perm.' When I clamped my lids really hard I could see us in the tub. Father imitating my giggle as I splash him in the face, mother all sweaty, scrubbing our heads and backs, washing dirty foam down with steaming water. My brothers are hiding all over the place to escape the Sunday bath. Mum cries, 'Come on boys, I haven't got all night!'

I can't possibly be remembering this. I was too small and my brothers were too big to let Mum wash them. Maybe it's just Father's story of our childhood wafting through my head. His voice. His face.

I caressed the sketch in the window and the image pulled a wry face.

Then a female voice itched my ears, 'She's crazy. I won't let my Jasmina sit close to her.'

'They killed them all. It's a miracle she's alive.'

'She doesn't look alive.'

I pressed my hands against my ears and counted to ten. As I put my hands down, the buzzing chatter invaded again and nobody's voice was clearer than any other's. I put my hand over my nose as if the sounds smelled bad, and somehow the sounds did smell bad.

I wrote my magic word *Dad* under the simple sketch and stared at it, waiting for it to begin dancing and then to leave me, betray me. I scowled at my reflection in the clean patches of the window and pinched my cheeks to see if there was still blood in me.

The bus stopped.

'Passport check,' the bus driver yelled. People became silent and started digging in their pockets and handbags as if they had no idea where they stashed their documents. The driver waddled down the aisle and gathered our red passports with yellow lettering, *SFRJ, Socialist Federal Republic of Yugoslavia*. He blew up his long Nietzsche-moustache and tapped me on the shoulder. 'Yours too, honey.'

'No.'

'What do you mean, No? I said—'

'No.'

He leaned over me, and hissed under warm, nicotine breath, 'Give me your passport or I'll kick you off the bus.'

I opened my handbag—my only luggage—took the passport from the top, slapped the man on his mouth, and gave him a gentle smile. He backed up and looked around the bus. People were still busy rummaging in their bags, making the sign of the Cross, muttering Quranic prayers, flicking rosary beads, or rubbing their passports for luck, all according to what creed sat closest to their hearts.

He folded my passport in the middle, continued down the aisle and went on hollering, 'Passports, please!'

I turned back to the window and looked out at the insouciant clouds. They had no boundaries to cross, their home a place so desolate it mocked destinations.

A boisterous voice made me lift my nose from the glass. 'Let's have a laugh! Come on, gather around me.' A hefty, wide-toothed woman walked by me and winked confidently, like an ancient, big-breasted statue coming alive. A moment later, a little group of men mustered in the back.

She said, 'Have you heard the one about Tito going to the States and forgetting the medals?'

A man who had come from the middle of the bus now sat at her feet and said, 'Tell us.'

'For God's sake,' his wife yelled at him from ten rows away. 'We've hardly left our country, and already you're making a fool of yourself.'

The hefty woman made herself comfortable and she winked at the couple of men who were waiting for her funny stories.

One of them, a scrawny man said, 'Come on, tell us a joke.'

'What do you like, honey?' She pinched his cheek.

For me, telling jokes was an art. I forget a joke as soon as I've laughed at it. My father loved political jokes—they gave the people a chance to have a say.

I stood up to see who was doing what. The woman signalled me to come and join them. I took a few steps closer and sat down at a safe distance from her. She spat in her palms, rubbed them against each other and commenced, 'You know how an American, a Russian and a Bosnian were tested to see if they could keep a secret?'

Her pack of men chanted, 'Tell us, tell us,'

'All three lads were told a secret, and then they were tortured, one by one, and I mean nasty shit, not some cultivated stuff like the truth serum.'

The man with a toothless gab giggled. 'I know that one.'

She slapped him lightly in the head and he shut up. 'So, the Russian lad threw in the towel after four days, the American after five, but after ten days the Bosnian was still silent. They couldn't bloody believe it. Our guy was adamant. So they stopped the procedure and went to his cell to give him the good news. They found our super-silent countryman banging his head against the cell wall crying out, "Remember you fool, remember, they'll fucking kill you! Why can't you remember?" '

I laughed and hit the seat edge with my head. The woman's mouth was like a sieve, all her energy just pouring through. I felt infected by the same germ. I wanted to cringe at her feet, embrace her rebellion.

I didn't.

'Did you hear the one about a sixty-year-old maid who was living alone in some Godforsaken village the Serbs pillaged?' The woman's eyes opened wide as she remembered that one. She wiped the sweat off her face and exhaled as if preparing to take a leap. The men came closer, almost climbing over one another.

'Well, the old maid heard about torches, guns, glistening blades, daylight thefts and above all, the raping of women. She was so overcome she wouldn't even cringe in a corner. She spent her time at the window, waiting for her fate. So when a Četnik plunged into her house, rifled through the place, took what little chattels she had and suddenly was on his way out, she cried out after him, What about the rape?'

They all laughed, and one man took a paper bag, put it over his mouth and panted into it. 'You're killing us.'

I stood up. Stiff. I moved towards the back of the bus. I could not quite see the woman. I saw a girl, as real as her, familiar, pale-faced and curly-haired, and my arms became big and hairy, and they pushed away the merry men and grabbed the woman's ears and threw her on the floor and I heard myself hiss, 'How about rape?' I tore open her blouse, exposing her breasts. She screamed. I hit her over the mouth with the back of my hand, yelling, 'Shut up bitch, I don't like noisy whores!' I pushed myself from her, sticking my hand between her legs as if I was trying to grab something and pull it from out of there. Her body bent as if her own stomach was trying to dislodge her from the floor, jerking her more and more until she shrieked and I shook my hand up and down above her face as if emptying a bottle on it. Someone pulled me away while I yelled, 'I told you to shut your mouth up, not your cunt! Open it! It's dry! I don't fucking like it dry!' Then I felt a smell of nicotine and a hit in my head

I woke up on another bus with a pulsating horn. An old woman I'd never seen before was combing my hair and holding a wet handkerchief over my bruised face. She recited short prayers as if to disperse evil spirits. 'Dear child, what made you do that?'

I did not speak, not even when we arrived in Świnoujście, Poland. I gazed at the harbour. There it was, a new border, wide and calm and blue, and on the other side of the fog was Ystad, Sweden. I wished I were the mythical Swedish giant Vist who tore off a part of land and threw it into a vast lake to make a crossing for his lady-giant.

Whispers sneaked from behind. I clamped my teeth shut and wished over and again Dad was there to scold me for what I'd done. Or, maybe he too would take revenge on the woman for ridiculing my pain. Maybe he'd tell me I was not the bad guy in this story.

The bus drove onto a ferry ship. Old, milk-smelling fingers combed my hair.

A wood of Christmas trees glistens in the evening light, then disappears when the bus enters the yard of the Uddevalla refugee camp. Two crescent moons rise in the naked twilight above two dirty-yellow buildings. It is cold, and the haze from my breath covers the window. Once more I draw my father's face: eyes, eyebrows, nose, and give him a smiling mouth. 'You look so funny, Mr. Storyteller. I love you even though you're dead, I love you more than anybody alive.'

I pucker my lips and kiss the forehead, giving it a third eye.

CONSULTATION WITH OXFORD ENGLISH DICTIONARY

refuge noun
1. [mass noun] the state of being safe or sheltered from pursuit, danger, or difficulty
2. [count noun] a place or situation providing safety or shelter
3. [count noun] an institution providing safe accommodation for women who have suffered violence from a husband or partner
4. [count noun] Brit. a traffic island
ORIGIN late Middle English: from old French, from Latin refugium, from Latin re- 'back' + fugere 'flee'.

refugee noun
1. a person who has been forced to leave their country in order to escape war, persecution, or natural disaster
2. [as modifier] refugee camp
ORIGIN late 17th cent.: from French réfugié 'gone in search of refuge', past participle of (se) réfugier, from refuge (see REFUGE)

home noun
1. the place where one lives permanently
2.an institution for people needing professional care or supervision
3. the finishing point in a race
[adjective, adverb, verb]
ORIGIN Almasa said, '?'

RED CROSS MESSAGE (UNADULTERATED)

From:
Almasa H. Omerović

To whomever it may concern,

It didn't happen in a day. It wasn't an impulsive reaction, even though THEY rushed into our homes like starving dogs. Nothing like that. At least not in my hometown. Bosnia is a small country, but the war had many faces. Enough stories to build another tower of Babel.

Everything started with renaming and prefix-ation. Everything was annexed to the word "Serbian", beginning with our mother tongue, and with it other words slid from it as if in an avalanche. The names of streets and municipal buildings mutated. My father started overusing this word and saying things like: 'Maria, would you please pass the Serbian salt? This Serbian beef and Serbian mashed potatoes and Serbian gravy are not salty enough. And while you're at it, some Serbian chilli would be great.'

I tried to copycat him, and I said, 'Dad, may I have some Muslim mustard with my Muslim hot dog?'

I wish he laughed.

The aggressors, armed with tanks and rotten reasons, knew we had no weapons, having confiscated the few hunting rifles that had been gathering dust in people's cellars. In the middle of it, we were still busy bickering about everyday things. Even the bloody footage from Croatia, followed by Sarajevo and other Bosnian cities, towns and villages, could not make us believe the war was really here to stay.

In the beginning, before the whole mess came to Bosnia, Father would not join the party and kill Croatians. My mum was Croatian. He lost his job and consequently, so did Mum.

Next came a curfew.

Going to the market to buy vegetables meant risking a beating.

Students harassed in schools.

Raids.

Insults.

Humiliation.

Razing of the mosques.

More beatings.

Body count.

Etc.

Still, nothing could make us believe it all was more than just an ephemeral whim of a malevolent wind, as some poet put it.

I put on my best shoes, stuffed my *Silver Surfer* comic, the one about hope and loss, under my blouse, my passport in my knickers, and fled.

Dad, Mum, seven brothers. They could not.

A dusty old bus took me through many beneficent countries that sheltered refugees from the Balkans. I didn't want to get off until I saw aurora borealis.

That is how I became a 'run-ee' or 'run-away-ee', as I nicknamed myself.

Cheers,
Almasa

MYTH OF THE SMELL

Sometimes I think the only real home for a refugee is an endless road. In second place, I don't know, maybe a bus. I feel like I've spent more time on different buses than in all the camps. Refugee camps, of course. These shelters end up in third place. I have nothing to put under number four. I don't seem to even have an All Time Top Five list.

But this, you already know. I will not offer you dull, simple stereotypes of the idea of a refugee. You need to hear something that elucidates the being of a refugee in a different way. This is not a parable or a metaphor, even though it might look like one. It's . . . I don't know, you'll see. This shows what it's like to be well accommodated in a foreign country and yet still long for a home to nestle in. And even though I view 'home' with suspicious eyes, I too have come down with a nauseating homesickness, which made me think I belonged to a people, not the Bosnians, but rather the race of refugees. The moment my bus mates left Bosnia, they chanted like little Dorothy, There's no place like home.

I was at first reluctant to describe the homeland, its fragrances, tints and textures. I just don't believe any refugee really has a clear memory of these things, but rather a vague feeling about something that might be causing our quirky behaviours.

At the beginning of our stay in this town Mullsjö, located between a muddy lake and an evergreen forest, we started off on a new life by facing a new language. The tongues of adults twisted and bent in desperate attempts to pronounce even three-word sentences. 'Oh, come on, for God's sake,' I used to tease them. 'Thank goodness we're not in China or Eskimo land. It'd take you ages to learn how to say, May I have some bread? Be grateful they have supermarkets here so you can just see where things are and take what you need, instead of asking for each item from the grocer sitting behind the counter.'

I exaggerated, of course. But you should have seen us, walking those clean, broad streets, unwilling to look at the scarce passersby, afraid they might ask us something. I guess the locals in this place hadn't had too many Gastarbeiter from the Balkans, so they told us we were surprisingly white for Muslims. Some of us were blonde and blue-eyed. Still, you could recognize us from a mile's distance: the ambling gait and the mismatched second-hand clothes, the lowered eyes and the hair styled by brain-numbing winds.

We improved.

I liked how the new hometown reflected in the lake, except in winter when it froze over and people drove cars across the ice to the other side where there was a hotel and an art school. The refugee camp was made of long, two-storey houses with four to six flats in each house, and only two families in each flat. Picture frustrated husbands, constantly smoking, whining about the good ol' days, and starving for news broadcasts: *Deutsche Welle, Radio Free Europe, Voice of America*; their dishwashing, food-cooking wives telling them to move their arses for once; kids taking every opportunity to watch MTV.

'Can you think of a worse place for a refugee than this?' I once asked Björn, one of the camp personnel, a curious man who liked walking among us. He'd left his factory job, his marriage, and all that jazz. He was trying his luck here.

'Of course I can,' he said, looking at me with ice-blue eyes. He looked almost like an albino. And straight from a Forties film, the hair bright and sleek, a Robin Hood moustache. He always breathed as if rushing somewhere. Smelled nice, though. Lemongrass.

I was afraid he had seen the question as proof of my ungratefulness, or a sign of some Slavic pride. I asked him what he meant.

'You know why. Because there is no place like home.'

I just gaped at him.

'I know what you're thinking. Such a cliché, huh? But I've been observing you Bosnians for a while now, and I just don't get it. I mean I do, but it seems to me that you love this—if you will excuse the expression—Bosnia, över allt annat, more than anything. You see, these last six months, now that the war's ended and all, I've seen people go back to their homeland and stay there for a month or two. In fact, they go as far as buying expired foods, digging for clothes in those yellow UFF containers, walking out on early Saturday mornings to gather empty cans and anything else to raise money for a bus ticket back. They tell me people back home expect them to come back with money as if they were Gastarbeiter.'

Since they did not defend the country, they should at least pay back something, I thought.

'When they return, they have a different zeal in their eyes and a feeling of disappointment at being here. I don't understand: why don't they just go back there for good?'

Because there really is no such place as home, I thought, and smiled. I used to tease my fellow countrymen for their homesickness, telling them if they longed for their hearths and doorsteps—oftentimes the only remnants of their burnt-down houses—why didn't they just pack their bags and leave this place where they had failed to find fertile soil for their roots? Boy, I hated those metaphors. I'd say, 'Bosnia is free now, so why not get the hell out of this paradise with apple trees and leaves big enough to cover your groin?'

Because we are cowards?

Or maybe because we, in our most intimate nooks, in our

à deux conversations, really do not believe there is a-place-like-home. We know that the moment we passed that booth with the sulky-faced border guard, our homeland was erased and turned into someone else's tabula rasa, left for others to carve the marks of their lives into it. I would tease them, but it would hurt me to see them purse their lips and mutter, 'You're such a killjoy.' And, with any indication of even the faintest thought that there maybe was nothing left to live for in Bosnia, sneers and suspicion—even from those who had begun to think in the same groove—would fall upon the turn-coat. Mine was not an easy confession.

The Swede continued, 'They always talk about Bosnian smells, how wonderful it feels to breathe there, while here they are choking. I find it so condescending. I love the way my country is. What is so much better about Bosnia?'

'She can tell you,' I said, pointing at Nijazeta, waddling towards us with a tray, three glasses clinking, lemonade running over their brims. Nijazeta is an old maid, as people have a nasty habit of saying, as old in face as the dress she's been wearing since she was a young woman. Childless, homeless, almost friendless, always shaky as if freezing, her eyelids only slightly swollen. She's been taking care of me for two years. Hers were the first pair of arms around me after my parents and my seven brothers died. I don't even know how. I hadn't been there to see their deaths, I was lying under a sweaty, panting slob, miles away.

'Nijazeta,' I said, as she shyly put the tray in front of us avoiding the guy's eyes. 'This man asks what Bosnia smells like. Could you tell him, and I'll translate?'

She sat down beside me, looked at the plastic table, then began to speak as if she'd been waiting for this opportunity all her life. 'Our houses smell of cold and fresh lime on early summer mornings after the regular spring white-washing. This pungent, tickling smell fades away a little every day thereafter. The summers pullulate with outdoor smells, budding trees of lilac, bramble, quince, plums, pears and apples. Meadow flowers bloom into wintertime. The wind never blows like it does here, incessantly, making you drowsy. They come and go, carrying the smells of seasons, eddying through space like Ramadan moves through time, sometimes moody like old people, sometimes just tired. Or strong, confining you indoors until you start sweating nervously. Or they disappear completely, to later breeze by when the worst heat comes over us.

'In winter, the lime evaporates stingily, fusing with the softly bitter smell of dry tree sap that seeps through the crevices of the stove, where it smoulders in burning logs like big incense. These then flow up and down in confluence with other plumes from the stove: veal and mutton, tomatoes, strong red paprika, beans, clove bits scattered over the hot plates, plum and pear compote, simmering milk turning into a fat crust at the surface that we eat with apple syrup and dark bread. These smells embrace cold afternoons and evenings, rubbing themselves against the cool air, as one would rub one's hands to warm up.

'These Swedish flats smell only of dirty wallpaper, linoleum floors that don't creak when you walk over them, and other building odours. These windows face only the walls of other buildings, or other windows with shades rolled down.'

Björn could hardly wait until I finished translating. He seemed to have understood what she was getting at from her face twitching, the oscillations in her breathing and the vehemence of her arm movements. 'But for Christ's sake, you're in a refugee camp. Our regular homes and yards have all the nice smells as well.'

'No, no.' Nijazeta flailed her arms. 'You just don't get it. It's, as people say, indescribable. Bosnian smells are special. They have a certain texture as they move in the air, like fine cashmere. They are sweeter, sourer, bitterer and mellower in their ripeness, like the greeting arms of a father.'

I caressed her cheeks. 'I think he's got it now.'

Björn was upset and tried to counter Nijazeta's patriotism.

He said, 'I've read that Bosnia is so war-torn now that streets are like fetid rubbish containers. Nothing works there. The locals dump garbage in rivers and abandoned backyards. They don't think the world of their country. They are hungry, jobless, and pissed-off. They'd leave at the first opportunity. But no country wants you now.' Then he heaved a breath as if he had swum up to the surface of our lake, and went on rumbling about everything that that just stank: corruption, drugs, something about his friends serving in the blue helmets—better known as Smurfs—who were constantly offered sex by young girls who reputedly wanted to get pregnant and so cheat their way out of the country. Even I could not listen to this, let alone translate it to Nijazeta. I sipped at my tasteless beverage, avoiding his eyes, giving him the deaf ear until he gave up and said good bye.

And that was all. It always cuts both ways. No winners or losers. Or maybe there always are losers.

My Swedish friend was right. In two ways. Such mythologizing and romanticizing of that little piece of land where we were—and did not learn to appreciate until now—is just silly. But he noticed one more important thing—it is an incurable condition. I asked him if there was a worse place for us than this, and he correctly answered, yes. A city would not be better than this forest town. It would bring back memories of the throngs of emaciated people in school gymnasiums and the high ceilings of religious buildings where we lived the first weeks as refugees (as if it were the beginning of a career). All the city stores and boutiques would speak of the things we didn't dare buy, for we had to focus on travelling light. Smells from street-kitchens would remind us we needed to eat too fast. No, a city would be an even worse refuge.

Still, wherever we are, there remains the *MYTH*, all defined, capitalized and italicized, built up from scratch into one of the most magnificent air castles between Heaven and Hell.

I wish my Swedish friends were there when Rabija came

back after a two-months' visit to her village in northern Bosnia. Then he would have seen how ridiculously homesick we could be.

Rabija's house was no longer occupied, and the government wanted her to register a request for her property to be returned to her. She needed to register as a returning refugee. So she hurried back to her place of birth to make sure the administration was working on her case. The authorities had assured her that her house would be emptied of the people then living in it and returned to her within a year or so, all according to the Dayton convention and the current mood in the neighbourhood. After completing all the paperwork, she kissed her rusty doorknob goodbye and returned to Sweden, even though she had no family here. She was hoping to get the money that the Swedish government had promised to the returnees.

As she stepped down from the train and into the Swedish forest, the camp folks gathered around her like bees around their queen, and asked what ought to be asked, 'What was it like?' What could it be like, other than what the Swede had described? But every time someone visited the homeland, everyone else spent the time biting their nails, anticipating news of the post-war home. The impressions of others would become their own.

Never did we hear about disappointments. Whatever was said was slanted over with the common closing sentence, 'What can I tell you, even the soil smells good back there.'

Then everybody would relax as if set free, exhaling a month or two of built-up expectations. They laughed and chattered, for a moment intoxicated by this happy message that the motherland itself had sent them, 'Tell them I'm fragrant. Tell them I'm sweet. Tell them I'm beautiful. Tell them I love them.' And a transparent amendment, 'Just don't send them back for a while, will you! I'm so damn tired.'

Rabija took her time. Reticent. Expressionless. Breathing ceased. Then she reached into the pocket of her washed-out cardigan and exclaimed, 'I brought you a piece of the land.'

I lunged forward and buried my nose in that piece of pale dirt and grass and heaved a deep breath. A second later I was pushed away. Everyone wanted to smell the piece of Bosnian soil that had travelled about three thousand kilometres and to rekindle his or her nostrils.

It had no smell whatsoever.

Then again, we knew it wouldn't. Still, everyone burst out, 'It smells wonderful,' and chattered for a moment about the peculiar qualities of Bosnian smells, and about how Bosnian food, its breads and meats, were sweeter than the dozens of varieties found in Swedish bakeries and shops. It was all as Nijazeta had tried to convey to the Swede.

What about the truth? I wondered and looked up the broad road to the refugee camp. I waved my hands. What about it? It doesn't smell good.

FIRST DAY OF NIGHT

Christmas Eve 1995. 11:34 a.m. The first time, Almasa says it slowly and softly, as if she is really looking for an answer, 'Are you talking to me?' She peers into the small, grimy mirror in a train toilet. She pulls the corners of her mouth down, making a true De Niro impression, and voices her question again, 'Are you talking to me?' She tries to turn her entire body around to look behind herself, like he did in *Taxi Driver*, but she only faces the door. The walls are so narrow they force her to stand with her back straight, the way her mother taught her girls should hold their bodies. Once again, she meets the mirror and stares at her moist pale face, the crescent-shaped swellings beneath her big black eyes, her lank hair. 'I don't see anybody else here. Do you see anyone else, motherfucker? What are you staring at?' She grabs her almost flat breasts and laughs. 'You like these? You want to rape me again, ha? Like last night and the night before, and the night before? Come on, you Serb chickenshit?'

She leans her temple on the mirror and says, 'Are . . . you . . . talking . . . to . . . me?' She starts sobbing, and then she dry heaves, but she cannot vomit, so she presses the brass-coloured button above the basin. A weak stream of water runs a few seconds and then stops automatically. She presses it again, catches some water in her hand, splashes her breasts and her white shirt glues to her skin. 'Yes, I'm talking to you, you pathetic little refugee.'

The train brakes, and despite the narrow space, her slim body folds like a clam shell, and her head hits the metal toilet. Without a sound, she resigns her temple to the cool and soothing metal, then the urine stench makes her jerk away, and she slams her forehead against the basin. 'Shit!'

There is an ear-ripping sound of train wheels, but Almasa imagines it is an old steam trumpet that announces her arrival to Kiruna, the northernmost town in Sweden, as close to the birthplace of Norse gods as a warm train could get her. This is a landscape under the spell of the polar circle and aurora borealis, the winter night dance of angels, from the first day of night until the first day of day.

Three days earlier Almasa was living in a refugee facility in Mullsjö. When the first snow arrived, the Swedish government threw gold-worth stay permits on all Bosnians, hela bunten, lock, stock and barrel. The big blonde and hairy camp manager Björn brought Almasa the good news. She jumped and tied her matchstick legs around him, and kissed his face as if the Green Card was a gift from him personally. Within forty-eight hours she had managed to rent herself a one-roomer in Kiruna, as far as she could go without losing every contact with the world. The safest place on earth.

11:47 a.m. Almasa steps off the train onto the empty platform and a midday night. The ground shimmers with weak florescent blue and yellow patterns, as if the sun left lingering traces in the hard snow and the station lights buzz buzz buzz, and then one bulb bursts. She holds an old-fashioned valise with a piece of her laced bra hanging out of it. To her right, there is a small Christmas tree with a too-big plastic star on top. The star twinkles, reflecting the faint light from the station window. It is crooked. Almasa walks over and corrects it. The star's weight pulls it down again and it falls down and bounces against the frozen concrete. She does not bother to pick it up again. She turns away and peers into the flat, open horizon, hoping, in a grand gesture, to imbibe the new, pristine world of the Arctic Circle, the snow-clean landscape. Her eyes hurt as if her look has bounced and pricked her pupils, and she closes them, but it does not help.

12:09. Almasa rubs her bare legs from her calves up to the edge of her short silken skirt, and then straightens to button her checkered wool coat. She lifts the collar high and ties it around her neck with a blue scarf. From her pocket, she produces a hand-drawn map of the town, on which she marked the address of her new place with a red pen. She looks up and says out loud, as if she is not alone, as if to some ghostly companion. 'That way.' On her map, the X-mark doesn't seem so far from the train station. She strolls and strolls and ambles, but does not reach the street she is seeking. She only circles around town blocks, which aren't really blockish but more like triangles with one corner chopped off, trapezoids, all kinds of shapes. After a while, she wants to believe she's managed to retrace her steps back to the station.

In what looks like the main street, all cosy and Christmassy, there is a pharmacy called the Swan. Swedish drugstores have animal names like that. Her icicle legs trip over themselves as if they are broken, and she drops her valise a foot from the window. She heaves a cold breath and, imagining she is being whipped like a mongrel, she drags her feet inside.

The small pharmacy is made of wood. Green-white decorations adorn the long desk that separates the waiting room from the shelves. The room smells of strong glögg, a hot spicy wine simmered with raisins and almond, which Swedes only drink during the holidays. Almasa follows the smell and spots a little iron cauldron hanging above a thick white candle, which keeps it warm.

'Please, help yourself. It'll do you good,' says a nice, old woman with a thick northern accent. Almasa smiles and thinks the woman must have once looked like a movie star. Under her formal attire, the woman still has firm breasts that ride high and proud like Scarlet O'Hara's or Bridget Bardot's. Almasa tries to keep a straight face and to rein in her thoughts. She lifts her gaze to the woman's ice-blue eyes and long lashes and says, 'Ah thank you. I'd love some. It's freezing out there.'

The woman looks at Almasa over her half-moon glasses. 'Poor thing, look at you. You're practically naked.' She squints, examining Almasa's face. 'You're not from around here. Are you a tourist? Your Swedish is good.'

The compliment makes Almasa's face tinge with warmth and she smiles. 'Sort of a tourist, but not any longer. I'm moving in here.'

The apothecary smiles and says, 'Welcome to the top of the world.'

'Thanks.' Almasa fills a small ceramic cup with glögg and leans on the counter. 'Do you have painkillers? And I mean killers.' She takes a sip and then shudders as the mulled wine splits into thin threads and coils around her limbs.

The apothecary disappears between some cabinets and returns with a box of Ipren. 'Here you go, varsågod. These are quite new and work fast. They will also warm you up, or help you with fever if you're sick.'

'Great. How much for these?'

'Fifty-three kronor.'

Before paying, Almasa tears the box apart, takes three pills and instead of swallowing them, she crunches them with her molars. She washes them down with her glögg.

'Hey, take it easy with these. One's quite enough.'

'Of course.' She uses her fingers to scoop out all the almonds and raisins from the bottom of the cup and eats them. Then she smiles at the woman, thinking she'd like to have breasts like hers. 'Thank you for the drink. Bye.'

'Hej då. God Jul.'

'God Jul.' Almasa feels a little awkward saying it back, as she always does. She's a Muslim and is not sure how she should feel about Christmas. She likes saying it to the Swedes though, a nice gesture of integration into the new community. Her father used to visit his Christian friends back in Bosnia on all their holy days, until the war, when he was taken from his friend's home at 05:01 one afternoon. She remembers the time, for she kept staring at the friend's cuckoo clock above the doorframe, as the soldiers were taking her, too. She counted seconds, tick tock tick tock tick . . . counting not up but down, sixty, fifty-nine, fifty-eight, tick tock tick.

Outside the pharmacy, she munches two more pills, and almost runs into three fat men in shabby clothes. They all have salt-and-pepper beards and they reek of all kinds of worldly stenches and they drag their Charlie Chaplin boots through the slush, heading toward the window of System Bolaget, a state-owned liquor store, the only place to legally buy alcohol. They blow their hot breaths against the glass and then press their faces up against the window. Almasa joins them, touching her own nose to the glass. It is dark inside. The men turn and look at her, their eyes moist and small. Almasa thinks, I shouldn't have taken so many painkillers, because her mind is either multiplying one single man, or maybe she is prejudiced and all Swedes still look alike to her, or maybe, when people spend every second of their lives living and drinking together they become like one, their skin grows into each other, personalities don't matter any longer, only the promise of long, strong swigs.

They say as one, 'Who the heck are you?'

She now can distinguish between them. Since their faces are overgrown with beards, she uses this system: the first man has a long nose, the second bulgy eyes, and the third has ears like Easter Island statues. She says, 'I'm Almasa.'

Mr. Long Nose says, 'That's a strange name. You a witch or something?'

'A witch?' She laughs.

Mr. Bulgy Eyes says, 'Why so merry?'

'I'm actually celebrating. I just became half-Swedish.'

Mr. Huge Ears says, 'Where's the other half?'

'Left it in Bosnia.'

They sing out in raspy voices, 'Ha, welcome to Sweden, kid.'

'Thanks. Appreciate it.'

'Would you like a drink?' Mr. Long Nose says, offering her a bottle wrapped in newspapers. His face wrinkles as he realizes the bottle is too light, and he peers sadly inside, turns it upside down, and not even a drop runs out. His disappointed eyes make her want to break inside the locked store and pick up a few bottles, mixing wine, whisky, and beer. Since she never drinks booze, she'd have no idea what to choose. Yet, for a moment, it seems like an awfully great idea. She pictures them all guzzling, first their throats warming, and then their entire bodies, and then the laughing and joking would begin, and then, then she doesn't know what comes next.

'I wish I could help you. I have some painkillers. That could be a Christmas treat.'

Mr. Long Nose tries to twists his bottle like a sponge, but it's still dry. He says, 'No, we don't need —' He stops when he hears the sound of a slowly-approaching car. A Beetle stops close to a tall and thick Christmas tree decorated with frosty lamps and a huge, frozen angel balancing on the top. A skinny, head-shaven teenager shoots his head out of the car's open window, hollering 'Kiruna FF,' which is the local football club.

Mr. Long Nose says, 'Totally out of season. Stupid spoiled brats. They don't know how to enjoy a drink, just guzzle anything like damn animals every weekend, and make noise.'

Almasa jumps up, her legs now defrosted, and runs to the car. The street is icy and she glides the last few feet and barely manages to avoid hitting it. The driver hollers, 'Are you mad?'

She smiles with friendly intent at the drunk, contorted face. She peers inside at the five additional red-nosed blokes crammed like sheep. The driver stares at her and says, 'What?'

'Hi guys. Can I steal some booze from you? Or, I can pay.'

The driver moves his eyes down to look at her legs and says, 'Come with us. We're going to this super cool party. You can get all the booze you want.'

'I just need a few bottles now, for my friends and me.'

He goggles at the homeless men, who are gulping like mad. 'You nuts? Those bastards? To hell with them.'

'Cut me some slack, will you? I'm new here. I'm freezing.'

Another guy opens his window and says, 'Can I see some ID?'

'What are you saying?'

He giggles, 'We are responsible, whatsitcalled, citizens, and we can't be caught selling alcoholic beverages to under-aged girls.'

She says, 'My God, thank you. You actually don't think I'm older than eighteen?' As so many times before, she pulls out her refugee camp card, looks at the ugly picture, and gulps. 'Twenty yesterday.' She laughs. 'I'd forgotten my own birthday. Now, I have two reasons for celebration.' Her eyes wander, and she isn't sure booze is the right thing, even though people in Bosnia always pull out a bottle when they say, 'Let's celebrate.'

She puts her ID against the driver's nose. 'OK, boys, what's it gonna be? We need something to drink.'

'What do you offer in return?'

She tips her head to the side and squints, trying to give the impression of Clint Eastwood's silent cowboy. Calm on the outside, a furnace in the gut, she thinks, Assholes. She flips open her coat, and flashes her flat tits. Snowflakes feel like hail hitting her skin. They howl. She closes her coat. 'All right, then?'

The driver hands her a half-full bottle of whisky, and two cans of beer called Pripps Blue.

She grips the bottle and dangles the beer from her other hand. 'Thank you.'

'Don't mention it.'

Off they drive. She can hear them still howling as they tear off down the street.

Almasa juggles the bottles, and proud-steps back to the men who have hungry, or rather thirsty, looks. They shiver with the same twinkling eyes as she gives them the alcohol, each takes a gulp of the strong stuff first, and they say in chorus, 'Herregud, you're an angel from heaven.'

The talkative Mr. Long Nose gives Almasa a nice stare and says politely, 'Do sit down.'

She slouches on the concrete block meant to stop cars from driving into the pedestrian walk, looks down the street that crumbles into dark fog, and says, 'You know, back in the camp, this shrink asked me what type of furniture I think I am.'

Mr. Big Ears takes large swallows of his beer and glances at Mr. Long Nose holding the whisky. He says, 'Shrink? What are you, a nutcase?'

She smiles.

Mr. Long Nose says, 'That's a crappy question, kid.'

'Exactly. That's what I said. I thought he was pulling my leg. Well, whenever I looked away, I felt he was pulling down both my long, colourful stockings, with his eyes.'

The men all stare at her naked, blue legs protruding from her open coat, and laugh. Mr. Huge Ears says, 'You have chicken legs, kid.'

Almasa hisses, 'You arsehole. I thought we were bonding here and now you're mocking me.'

He shrugs, and says, 'You broke the ice girl, right?'

'All right, all right.' Almasa folds her arms around her legs and straightens her back. 'Now I lost the track, oh yes, what kind of furniture am I? I think I now understand the point. It strikes me that I'm no domestic thing, no furniture. I might be this grey concrete on which we are sitting.'

The men try to bend forward to check the concrete under their behinds, but their large stomachs are in the way. Mr. Enormous Ears says, 'You really are crazy.'

'Ah, forget about it.'

Mr. Long Nose gives her a sad look and shoves the bottle of whisky into her hands, then immediately changes his mind and takes it back. Instead, he snatches the beer from

Mr. Huge Ears, takes a swallow, and then gives her the rest, which is not more than a sip or two. His friend's chin drops, but he says nothing.

'Thanks.'

'Cheers.'

Almasa retches at the foamy beer, puts the can down, and grabs the whisky bottle from Mr. Long Nose's grasping hands. She holds it close to but not against her lips, and pours small portions of the burning liquid. She spits it out.

He brawls, 'Hey girl, give it back! It's mine! Watch it so you don't spill!'

The others start yelling too. She ignores them and swallows little by little. The combination of tiredness, whisky and pills should equal double intoxication, as they taught her in the driving school, being tired is the same as being wasted. Almasa retches again as the booze lingers in her throat and drops into her stomach like hot coal. She empties the bottle onto the frozen asphalt and it becomes darker as the ice thaws. 'No more drinking, boys.' She knows it is the nastiest thing she could do to them, giving them a gift and showing it is really hers to take back.

The men shake like jackhammers, and they want to jump up and kick her butt, but the only thing that rises is the blood rushing through the crackled capillaries in their faces.

She says, 'Do you guys know how I can get myself to —'

They holler, 'Jävla lilla hora. Satans jävla helvete.'

Almasa laughs and says, 'Ah, that doesn't fucking scare me. I've been called a whore by real motherfuckers before. You three are nice.' She thinks Swedish must one of the poorest languages in the world when it comes to swearing. To use knulla (fuck) in Swedish would sound unidiomatic.

The three drunkards continue to grumble. Almasa shrugs her shoulders, gets up, and ambles down the street, leaving the men to their muttering. She tries to ask passers-by for directions. A couple of blonde beauties in trench coats shrug their shoulders and walk away, giggling. A guy dressed like

Run DMC says, 'Yo, sure I know, I've got a couple of cool dawgs in that hood, they're really digging my beat, you know what I mean.'

Almasa thinks the world is really small. She never thought she'd meet such different people so far north. She says, 'Of course. Just point.'

'You can take the bus.'

'I hate buses.'

'Well that's the only—'

'Just point somewhere. My map sucks.'

He looks at her hand drawing, and guffaws before he gives her an appraising look. 'Man, you're cool. Wanna walk? Alright, you want to go to the end of this street and then turn right into a smaller street and follow it until you see a church. Walk toward the mountain you see far away. If you're lucky, you'll barge into someone who can tell you the way from there.'

'Aren't you a pal?' She presses her lips hard against his naked chin.

He smiles and blushes. 'Cool.'

He leaves and Almasa watches him with a smile. Every now and then he turns around. She tries to blow him another kiss but her hand is shaky, and she cannot bring it to her mouth.

She does as he instructed, and she wishes she wasn't so stupid, or drunk, or tired, or all of these states. The traffic is not too bad. A few cars now and then wake her up from her walking trance, mostly Volvos and Saabs, big bulky cars. One has bars in the back, behind which there is a dog with a long, watery tongue flapping against the windshield. She snaps her eyelids open at the soft light and mellifluous sounds from a big, bright church. Swedish Christmas songs set the cold air vibrating. The church is earth-coloured and looks like a chopped top of a wooden mountain. Almasa continues down the street, through a patch of woods and then over flat, frozen meadows, whistling a tune.

An hour later, a police officer parks his motorcycle a few

yards in front of her. He comes to her slowly and buoyantly, like a motorway poet, looking for inspiration in the real world. He takes off his helmet and the black goggles. For some reason, she expects long hair à la Samson to fall over the tight, leather jacket. Instead, he is old and bald, but has nice blue eyes, and an honest smile. He looks nothing like her father, yet, at that moment, if she had never seen the burnt face of her dead dad, she'd swear to God he was walking again to meet her with his arms stretched out, touching east and west.

'Miss, it's a little silly to walk on the motorway, isn't it? Can I assist you home?' The word he uses for silly is knasigt, which she heard once before in a crash course in ceramics that her shrink had recommended she take as a form of therapy, to immerse herself in something practical instead of constantly dwelling in her raving brain. The pottery teacher used the word knasigt for the colour that didn't come out right after burning.

She says, 'I missed you so much.'

He turns around, then back. 'Are you talking to me?'

She winces as his words pull her from her reverie, and says, 'I don't see anybody else here.'

'Let's go to the station and—'

She gives the officer a crumpled piece of paper with an address on it. She shows him the map and points in the direction he should drive. He laughs so much that the tiredness disappears from his eyes. She tries to swing her leg up and mount the bike, but her knee hits the back wheel. He helps her up. She sits behind him and buries her fingers in his uniformed stomach. The experience of the drive is what she expected: cold wind cutting her face and legs, a revving engine reminiscent of the powerful bike with more equipment than Spielberg used in *ET*.

She does not kiss this shining knight when he drops her off in front of the house where she has rented a room. She watches him zooming off and shudders, but not from cold.

Uniforms still make her body remember the violence. The three-storey-high building looks like an abandoned doll's house. Almasa thinks it is strange there are not even typical advent candles in the windows, or star-shaped lamps. She rings the bell but no one comes out. She thinks, They must be in church, and she checks under the flowerless pots for an envelope she was told would be there in case they were not home when she arrived. She picks the purple envelope up and tears it open. Two small, old-fashioned keys fall on the concrete. She waddles up one flight of dark stairs. She does not know which door is hers so she tries all of them until one opens. She takes a half step in. A maw of chlorine-smelling emptiness swallows her and she cringes by the door and shivers.

Hours later, she can hear the other tenants returning and the merry voice of the landlady. She imagines lights coming on, but she does not let her know she has arrived.

She stays there until the morning, which is just as dark as the midnight hours. Then she goes out. She hears three kids laughing, and follows the sound until she sees two boys in winter overalls, and a black girl with a scarf around her head and a wool hat on top of it. They are making a snowman. Almasa ambles over to them and kneels by the snowman. She says, 'You know what, I have the mind of winter, too.' The kids stand beside her and stare. She hugs the snowman as hard as she can, kissing its carrot nose and coal eyes. The poor thing crumbles in her warm embrace.

The children yell like mad in languages she doesn't understand. They make snowballs, put pinecones into them, and hit her in the head. She doesn't resist. She closes her eyes and falls into the snow and makes angels while the kids are bombarding her.

When they tire and leave her, she stands up and watches the flat horizon with an enormous black peak cutting right into the sky. A few yards from her, between the pine trees, walks an old, hunched woman with a brocaded scarf on her head. Almasa immediately recognizes the old-fashioned Bosnian outfit and thinks, There's no escape from the past. She was hoping to never again see a countryman, or woman. The sky is clear and streaks of light gather above the mountain and slice the dark background with green and blue leaves of light. The northern lights look as if they are setting on the old woman's head, or as if they are welling out of her tiny body. She looks mystical and mythical, both native and strange. Almasa cannot see her face but feels like running to her and hugging her. The uncanny spectacle of the sublime landscape and the weak female body make her warm for a moment. The woman disappears. Almasa smiles, laughs, guffaws and goes back to her room thinking, I'm in the right place.

INTEGRATION UNDER THE MIDNIGHT SUN

For three years I have been embalmed, but there is faint thunder under my ribs. I wear the same outfit in which I left Bosnia: a blue oversized cardigan somebody wrapped around me that night I was shoved into a bus for Sweden, a pink shirt and a white bra with laced edges underneath, a short, corduroy skirt and mismatching colourful stockings, like the ones of Pippi Longstocking.

I bask in the midnight sun, which is colder tonight than usual. The polar circle is gliding down to this town. I do not want to go to my one-roomer. I have nothing there but two half-withered plants named Adam and Eve, sheltered behind metal shutters, cut off from all the temptations of nightlight. When they are not placed next to each other, Adam and Eve produce drops of water on their thick leaves—tears of separation. But these two specimens are crying all the time, as if they have been unhappily married since naked times.

It would be nice to have a house like the one back home in Bosnia, but what good would it be if it was not crowded by my parents and seven brothers. There would be no steam from the kitchen, no thick smells of exhausted bodies. I used to tell them apart by the sweat on their cheeks and necks and backs, by the way it mixed with the soap smell from their uncombed hair and their hand-me-down clothes. In the mornings, I would lie in my bed, pretending to be asleep until each and every one of them gave me a kiss. They would whisper, 'Snow White, rise and shine.' Waking up, the splendid ceremony.

Not any more. I wake up alone and the first face I see is my own. The mirror tells me my hair is no longer jet black; there are lime-white, unwieldy streaks on my head, but my skin is still fair.

It is 1996, and all quiet on the home front: father gone, mother not near. Only, in my tale, there are no stepmothers or stepfathers, or even stepbrothers. They are dead. So I have heard. The house was razed. So they keep telling me. Nothing changed a bit. So I go on dreaming every night.

I pray pray pray to dream of my family awash in blood, butchered and heaped on one another. But I can only see them gathered under a bright, sunless sky, I can see the crown of an giant chestnut tree in the middle of a dark-green pasture, and my brothers beckoning me to come and sit down as if they are taking a picture for the album, for a fixed future instead of memory, even now when I crouch in a laundry room waiting for my clothes to dry, they push my reflection from the washing machine glass and sit tight together watching me, smiling laughing guffawing.

'Disgusting,' I yell at them. 'How dare you? How can you just turn up before me like that, clean and without a scratch—happy? Why are you smiling? You smile as if that means something. It means nothing!'

The two Swedish women behind me stop whispering about the scars on my buttocks, and inch out. I can hear their peevish voices and want to tear out their bloody tongues, but a feeling strikes me and I can see myself turning into one of them. I take the wet clothes out of the rotating drum and dress. The clothes stick to my skin. I run to the one place where I can find peace, to Aziza and the incessant chatter of a group of women talking into each other's mouths. There, I am not the subject, the protagonist.

Aziza is a frightfully lean, seventy-year-old creature from Srebrenica. Her clothes have red-rose embroidery over bright, pastel colours. A veil borders her bony face, her pointy nose red like a soft cherry. Her puppy eyes are always moist, shyly shifting around, as if afraid to be caught looking too long at one and the same thing. She gives the impression of a jolly drunkard taking it easy for a moment. Not a nice thing to say about such a pious woman, but I love her too much to make her a stereotype.

Aziza is living alone. Her small flat is like Srebrenica, whose female inhabitants are scattered all over the world like shiny dots you can see in those satellite photographs of the Earth at night. Srebrenica is no longer a town, a real place, it comes to reality as a pattern that appears only when all these shiny dots are joined by a line, the pattern of the worst crime in Europe since WWII. The all-too-familiar pattern, every war's cliché that constantly survives the muddy boots of time.

Aziza had five sons and not one daughter. Her boys happened to have sons, too. A daughterless family. Nowadays, sonless as well.

She often tells me she has been thankful for the sons, but her fingertips never fail to tremble when she adds the old Bosnian myth that every corner of a house sings when a daughter is born in it. I had heard this saying a couple of times as a child and I had always found it mysterious, and gentle too. I had to come to another country and meet Aziza to find out why: 'Because the house knows that its support is not pillars and earth, but a woman's back.'

Now that she is so old and has no one to take care of, Aziza devotes her time to prayers. In spite of all her misery, she is the liveliest person I have ever met. She can cheer you up just by looking at you with those mellow eyes. She recites the Quran mellifluously and knows all things religious. People say she is an Awliyah, God's precious friend. Everybody loves her and there is not a single person who does not respect her, even those who normally do not like old, pious people.

Women and men, well, mostly women, come and ask for her help. Lots of them do if they have difficulty making decisions, marriage problems, love grievances, lost valuables, all worldly matters.

But Aziza is not a fortune-teller. She cannot peer into the future. All she does is pray a special prayer called istihara. The answer comes in a dream. But she never bothers interpreting it. She just says, 'Those are not my dreams. They belong to those who have asked for keys, clues and signs.'

Aziza has prayed a great many istiharas for herself as well, to get news about her sons. For too many years they have been missing. Dead? Alive? But every single time she wakes up after a dreamless night as if she has been praying in vain.

The evening I come to Aziza, there are at least a dozen women there, talking, crocheting, singing, laughing, and then when old memories come over them, crying, cursing.

A woman, the only one dressed up and wearing make-up, scolds her friends as if they are small children, 'Back in Bosnia, we worked hard, never got rich for that, but women didn't go around with their hair messy. Here nobody cares. For the love of God, I hear women back there look better now than you do here, in peace and prosperity.'

I sigh, enjoying the invisibility of being there, like an oar in warm lake water. The old Aziza has no satellite dish, so evenings at her home are absolutely news-less; she knows that the kind of news she needs will never be broadcast.

Bosnian women love these short disconnections from the reality of Bosnia and other troubled worlds of which they are constantly reminded by every single TV or radio broadcast. Bosnian men are obsessed with news; they even listen to news in languages they do not understand. A morning piece of news is mulled over and over until the last BBC broadcast at midnight, after which they finally go to sleep.

I search Aziza's eyes. They are almost closed. She looks cuddled in her sand-coloured veil that is falling over her eyebrows. I feel my own lids sinking down beneath the buzz of female voices.

'Ha, I can tell you about rubber hats,' a high-pitched, glassy voice says, cutting short the ongoing chatter and my nascent slumber, summoning all eager eyes to old Latifa. She is tall and forceful, so there is always empty space around her for her hefty gesticulations. She straightens her back, flails with her big hand and begins, 'After twenty years of marriage and seven children, my husband comes to me one night with this rubber hat on his little prick and wants to try some birth control. 'Birth control, my arse,' I say. 'After I've borne you five girls and two boys, oh no, that thing is not going into me. Over my dead body.' I hit his thing with the remote control so he never again thinks of putting me on like that.'

Latifa has a serious expression on her face, but the rest of us cannot hold back laughter.

A question pops out from somewhere, 'Didn't you bear more children after that?'

'Just one more daughter.'

Everybody guffaws. I hold my hand over my mouth and nose.

'You just laugh, but when I was your age and newly married, I didn't dare ask my mother-in-law anything, but she did tell me once that what was in my heart would come out of my belly. I bore child after child till I started to mix up their names, then I stopped.'

One woman laughs so much she falls on the floor.

'What are you doing?' Latifa leans over her and slaps her playfully across the mouth.

Only Aziza looks unmoved, except for an occasional contented smile. Her hands are stretched down over her knees like on an ancient guardian sculpture, the cracks and crevices in her features holding traces of old winds and ancient rains. To watch Aziza's beautifully wrinkled eyes and dimples is like drinking from a cold well whose water freezes your innards so much it feels hot and burning. I ask her how many evanescent hours she spent in crocheting that flower pattern on her scarf.

'Oh, I don't know. It was long time ago. It isn't pretty I know, just the everyday one I had on my head when I left Srebrenica. You should've seen a shawl I bought on Haj. Sewn with a golden thread. But I don't care. I don't miss anything: house, orchard, or clothes, not even Bosnia. God's earth is large, and there is room enough for everybody. These good Swedish people just gave us everything, and what have we done for them. If my family was here with me . . . ' She stops there, turns around and smiles at some women having an argument. It strikes me Aziza must be the best-integrated refugee under the sun.

This evening nobody has anything they need help with, so after hours of talking with everybody and chanting along with others in her smooth voice, Aziza slumbers. I sink deeper into my chair.

Then, Aziza winces. Only I see this moment. It is not even a moment. It is just our faces close to each other, like two leaves, moist and smelling bitter in the hot room, caressing each other without touching. Her lids open. She smiles and says, 'Elhamdulillah.' Then she dozes off again.

Before I can even think about what just happened, there comes a knock at the door. It is the husband of one of the women. He looks confused but manages to say 'Merhaba,' and inquire of everybody's health. His wife jumps up from a chat with her neighbour. 'The minute we gather for some gossip you men have to ruin everything! What are you doing here? I can't always take care of everything, you know.'

He gathers himself and looks right through her, saying, 'I came to see Aziza. It's urgent.'

'Have you lost your mind? And want her to find it?'

'Please. I have news to tell her.'

'What could a man come with, if not news?' some of the women whisper too loudly to one another.

Everybody turns to Aziza. Gently, a girl nudges her shoulder. Nothing. Then, as if after a failed joke, silence spreads in the room, silence that speaks more than a thousand pictures. My eyes blur. Everybody's do.

Then the man starts crying as well, his tears fall down without even touching his face.

'Please stop that,' his wife says.

He doesn't.

Latifa says, 'Well, tell us.'

He puts his hands over his face and when he removes them, he says, 'Just an hour ago, a man was visiting the Bosnian club, he is the manager of an excavating team financed with international money to search for mass graves and identify the bodies of the victims. He was in Sweden to tell us about his work in eastern Bosnia and to give information he had about the missing people. On his list of the identified bodies, he had the names of every single man from Aziza's family.' The man sobs. 'I knew this was not good news, but I know Aziza would've given everything for any news, good as well as bad. I failed her, and she died with half her heart.'

I clamp my lids shut and they empty like small bowls. I hide my face behind my pale hands, so nobody can see my smile. I smile with Aziza. I know why I should. Somehow, the news has been delivered.

I walk out and keep my eyes wide open as I bask in the midnight sun all the way back to my flat. I do not even find ghosts there. Just my happy couple Adam and Eve. I touch them; their leaves are dry like powder and so is the soil. I put the pots into the bathtub, jump in myself and we all take a long shower. The beating of the falling water makes me drowsy. My family turns up out of the fumes. They are swimming in the little river just a mile from our house. My father plummets from the willow that grows out of the cliff above, and dives all the way to the waterfall where I am hiding. He cries, 'Look what I found here!' He pulls me out and throws me amidst the rest.

MIND'S GARBAGE

I confess . . . I admit . . . no, that's no way to kick off a relationship with you. Here, you get a kiss for not rolling your eyes. Let me just apply some crimson lipstick to these cherry lips, ahhh, there you go, now, here comes the kiss. And now comes my Top Ten, no, my Top Eleven list, of what, you wonder? Well, let me take an awfully long time to introduce myself, before I grant you access to my list. I mean, I bet you have a list, all kinds of lists. I have been making lists since *High Fidelity*, only longer. Top Five? Huh, you don't fit anything into five, it's more like grading scale back in Bosnian schools.[1]

Right now I'm no more than a scrapbook, a damn shoebox full of notes on yellow Post-it squares, or three-ply toilet paper, cut-out corners of tablecloths, napkins, the insides of tampon boxes with scribbles from edge to edge. A collection of pieces from different jigsaw puzzles.

There's also a well-rounded ME, described in a whole lot of short stories. You see, I was tricked into being the protagonist in fiction. I still don't know how to pronounce that damn title, [Refuge]e. I gave the author a terrific piece of amateur editorial advice to change it to *Memoirs of a Bosnian*, or even add 'Nervous Wreck' Bosnian. 'Trust me, that'll sell,' I said pointing my thin, nail-eaten-to-the-quick finger at his left eye. The wretched wannabe writer gave me the cold shoulder, and left out all the quirky but fine incidents of my

---

1.   In Bosnia, we were graded 1 for fail and 5 for excellence.

life. So much was taken from me by the war already, my virginity for instance. Then he just chucked half my life into a kind of mind's garbage.[2]

He said, 'I must have some logic and linearity.' My God, as if I was testifying in the Hague against war criminals, who, by the way, hadn't been caught anyway, and couldn't afford to be contradicting or have out-of-character traits. So it's my turn to do it myself. Why let anybody else make your life into art. The idea makes me sick to death. On a pitch-black Swedish winter morning, I like this scrappy-ME better. In these stories, I was described, or rather served to you like a heavy dinner, not a light breakfast in bed, or some such thing. Yes, I was described, through a variety of expressionistic stories, as a Bosnian, a rape victim who has lost her whole family (dad, mum, seven brothers), a victim who fights not to be a victim, who struggles to be taken for her other qualities, one of which is her violent nature, propensity to existential angst, her utter hate of racism and nationalism, inability to connect with people her age (or younger or older), cynicism. 'Nuff said.

Below follow my own outtakes, like those which film directors gather up and put on an extra DVD alongside extended cuts, director cuts, CO cuts, the janitor cuts. I know, I know, I too buy those double, triple, quadruple DVD boxes, but boy do I get disappointed. I say 'disappointed' like Kevin Kline in *A Fish Called Wanda*, which, by the way, had really nice extra footage, so buy it. Have you ever considered that watching the Special Features feels like having the waiter come up to you after a terrific meal and ask if you'd be interested in having the scraps that the cook didn't use in the final version of the dish you just devoured like a starving animal, I mean I eat like that, not very feminine, whatever. Imagine a waiter not unlike John Cleese from *The Meaning of Life* with a bucketful of onion peels and potatoes, eggshells and cellophane, miscellaneous bones and paper tissues swimming in burnt

2.   I stole this phrase from Alice Munro.

oil and the water in which he washed his hands.

But, if you're a sucker like me, imagine lying awake in the wee small hours, hearing the raspy voice from American trailers saying, 'Meet Almasa.' Almasa is my name; sorry I forgot to tell you earlier. The man goes on, 'She's everything you fear to meet. She's your worst nightmare. But one man will solve the mystery. One man will tame the brawling Bosnian beast. *Almasa: The Movie*. Now on Double Disc Wide Screen Edition' in HD so you can't miss any tints, textures or hefty gestures.

Where was I . . . yes, linearity, important to follow . . . ah yes, mind's garbage. My problem has always been that I accomplish the opposite of what I want. When I try to be complex, I become flat. When simplicity and subtlety is my latest attempted virtue, I start bustling like some Middle Eastern market. Never been to one though, but I've heard of them, read about them, seen a picture or two in a magazine. No woman is a market, anyway. Even if I were, I'd still need a place for the garbage.

In another era, I would have been a simple dustbin, but, since I'm a modern woman and in these modern times we recycle everything so as not to hurt nature, I'll try to sort my life into different containers so that others, God knows who, can perhaps make use of these leftovers and preserve the environment. We never really reuse our own garbage ourselves. There are other wretches of the Earth who get to do the dirty work.

I will try to order my garbage thematically, or even organically, top-to-toe.[3] I will select 11 middle-sized containers in different colours and neatly organize everything this author didn't use in the stories about my life, as in "A Woman Already not Young," which in the original had a fancy title in French, just in case some super educated literary critic one day picked it up and said, 'This title is a direct reference to the French philosopher blah blah blah.' I have even forgotten

---

3. Speaking of feet, this sentence is a bit awkward, isn't it? Never mind, let's keep it.

which one Adnan Mahmutović was trying to refer to. It feels like such a total waste of effort to put in a reference hardly anyone would ever get.

Anyway, finally, your patience has borne fruit, the top 11:

1) Paper and Cardboard
2) Hard plastic
3) Soft plastic
4) Coloured glass
5) Non coloured glass
6) Metal
7) Batteries
8) Wood
9) Clothes
10) Food
11) Objects too large to fit into any of the above. Eleven is like an amendment to the ten commandments of my scrappy life.

1) Paper and Cardboard. Pink Container.[4]

I never use napkins or handkerchiefs to wipe my nose. I so much love their beautiful textures and pictures or abstract patterns, and have ever since I was a girl and my friends and I collected them back in elementary school. Ironically, if these napkins were not so nice, then I wouldn't want to use them at all. I would be a damn snob who wipes her snout on her sleeve. I'm not sure I should have said this at all. At least not right off the top, but this is my mind's garbage.

2) Hard Plastic. Yellow Container.

One winter morning, I was returning from Swedish for Beginners class, my head swollen with thoughts about positive integration and the mixing of cultures, people from different backgrounds all living in suburbia and hating each other's guts, and other such clichéd concerns of a young immigrant bird like me. Suddenly[5], a group of boys and girls

---

4.   I know it is incorrect to mix the two, but I just can't be bothered to separate them.
5.   I have to say I don't like using this word 'suddenly'. I've stopped using it, but here it obviously must be together with the remains.

attacked me with frozen snowballs to avenge their destroyed snowman, which I had unintentionally hugged to crumbles after my first and last drinking session with the downtown homeless people. I never had a drop of alcohol after that incident and I was glad the kids snowballed me.

3) Soft plastic. Brown Container.

I'm a real softy. Once a month I sit in a children's playground watching the little things mess around. I weep inside, but keep my face dry as if training to be a Spartan mother. Yesterday, though, this skinny girl came to me and put her sandals on the bench where I was sitting. Then she took out a few coins and said, 'Can you take care of these things for me? I'll be right back.' I said, 'All right, I'll keep an eye on the valuables.' She dashed away but then returned immediately, took her stuff and disappeared. A minute later, she came back with a bag of liquorice sweets and fed them to me. I hate that disgusting candy. It always makes me tearful, dammit.

4) Coloured glass. Black Container.

When I started high school, a teacher we called Methuselah Mehmet recited an old epic about this vagabond and thief who used to attack some prim queen's delivery boys, like some Balkan version of Robin Hood. Anyway, in the poem, the man was captured, then tortured in the most horrible ways, but he would not divulge the secret whereabouts of his gang. He said, 'I won't talk,' and tried to spit but he was too weak so he only spat on his chin. The queen herself stuck large rusty spikes under his nails. The teacher said, 'Whoever tells me why she did it won't have to lift a finger for the rest of the term, and will still get a 5. The possibilities: because he was a thief, because he was a hero, because he was a terrorist and she wanted to find his stash of weapons of mass destruction, because .... You get the point.' I said, 'Because she loved him.' Everybody thought it was a perverse thing to say, but Mehmet nodded and smiled at me. Now how is this part of my personality? I'm not sure. I'm still a bit kinky. Ah, I know, it's because I thought I'd be a great academic, but ended up being . . . something else.

5) Non-coloured glass. Purple Container.

Methuselah Mehmet told us about an old priest called George Herbert who couldn't pray except when set on fire by a shooting star. My father told me to tell Mehmet it was William Blake. I did. Then Mehmet said my father was an ignorant peasant. I told my father and he said that I should say to Mehmet that a man can be mistaken about something without being called an ignorant peasant and that he should go and . . . . Here father stopped and never finished the sentence, but I thought it was finished so I gave the message to Mehmet, who obviously filled in the gap, which I at the time could not understand, and he bereaved me of my hard-won victory, I mean the grade I got for interpreting that poem. My father was furious, mounted a bike and rode away. The next day Mehmet sang another song.

6) Metal. Blue Container.

To cut a long story short, I used to make small nicks on my thighs with forks. I didn't have a favourite fork, but liked to change forks from time to time. We didn't have any silverware or gold forks, so after I'd exhausted the range of implements available at the low-class level we clung to, I just stopped. My obsession with change put an end to my tendencies.

7) Batteries. Orange Container.

Last year I married this Somali man, Ibrahim. I first met him some sixteen months earlier when I was waiting for bus 420 to Stockholm University where I work as a research fellow in English Literature. I was so attracted to him I wanted to jump him right there at the bus stop, but he was new to Sweden and could hardly put together two words of Swedish, so I used body language, wink wink, you know what I mean. Next morning, I slid some extra padding in my bra. I put triple layers over my skinny behind, because I figured African men liked big bums. The communication was perfect. I showed him the picture of the Somali bankers from Stockholm accused, without a shred of evidence, of having financed Al Qaeda, and whose bank had been shut down. I shrugged my shoulders and said 'Life's a bitch, ain't it?' He smiled and nodded like a schoolboy, staring at my long neck and my cleavage. I winked again, but then he explained he was a pious Muslim. I said I was, too. Then, his face flooded in sweat, he said we'd have to get married first. 'All right, big boy,' I said in Bosnian, the following Friday morning, when I busted open the door of the classroom where he had his Swedish for Beginners lesson and dragged him to a local tailor who fixed him up with a nice jacket and a tie. Then we found an imam who could perform a quick joining of good souls.

8) Wood. Grey Container.

Ibrahim is great in bed. I love him. He's a keeper.

9) Clothes. Well, another Grey Container.

I never wear a bathing suit when I take dips in the nearby lake.

10) Food. Green Container (of course).

Now I have to take another risk. Ever since I came to Sweden, I've stopped eating. Or, I mean, not stopped, like being anorexic or bulimic, as is fashionable these days. I just don't really pay any attention to tastes, that's all. I eat anything. I have become a vulture of a kind. Since I eat anything, except for the bones that my dog eats, I have nothing to put out with the garbage. I'll just leave some blank space on this sheet, empty like a roaring stomach. You can put anything in this slot. Take a pen and fill it in.

{

} This should be about enough.

11) Objects too large to fit into any of the above categories. (I have run out of containers so I'll just, well, I actually have no idea what to do with this.)

p.s. Ah, who cares about p.s.

MIDSUMMER.
IT'S RAINING

I had a dream. Midsummer night's dream. I became a real Swede, eating small strawberries in the midsummer rain, leapfrogging in circles around a goat made of hay with a red ribbon around its neck, and fucking a drunken stranger in an unfamiliar house. I was too polite to ask if it was a man or a woman. Yes, I was that drunk.

I'm a woman, by the way. Born and bred.

I always try to reconstruct the sex I've had under the influence, and maybe some of the grand prelude, if there ever is any.

This time it all played out on a private island in Stockholm archipelago.

I was sitting at a plastic table with paper plates and paper cups with white wine. Was it half-full or half-empty? Can't remember. A child was whining in the background over the silly song called 'This is my life, my friend,' the Swedish contribution to the 2010 *Eurovision Song Contest*.

Someone said to me, 'Happy birthday.'

I turned around. A curly-haired person, with a nose that would make any witch envious — minus the hairy wart — was giggling close to my face. Thin lips. Mouse-teeth. I rubbed my eyes as if that'd compensate for the loss of my thick glasses, which I'd dropped into the lake on the way to this island.

'How do you know it's my birthday? Did Måns tell you?'

'Who's Måns?'

'The friend of the friend of the owner of this place.'

The curly-head shrugged.

'Never mind. But honestly, how could you know?'

'You're not having fun. You sit and munch those shrimps and strawberries and swig at schnapps like someone who has no one on the most important day of the year.'

I put down my fork with the shrimp on it. 'That's bloody uncanny. You're gifted.'

'I can also tell you're Bosnian, but with a nice Kiruna accent, which means you came here very young, but not young enough. You might have been through stuff, so I'm assuming that's contributing to the more general darkness in your aura.'

I pointed at his robe, or dress, or whatever you call those big white garments with flowers and curlicues. 'You're like a freakish, Hare Krishna Sherlock.'

'I'm Thomas DiLeva. A musician. A spiritualist. A lover.'

'Almasa. A rape victim.'

'Nice to meet you, beautiful. I hope this negative experience of yours hasn't, how to put it, made you reluctant to experience the pleasures of love.'

'No. I quite like fucking. I fuck anything that moves.'

'I sense a certain hostility. Something I've said?'

'No. Just the way I am. The darker version of Shakespeare's dark lady.'

'Can't stand that bugger.'

'Really? Come on. There's not much meaning to life if you take good old Shake it baby out of the picture. Quoting him works wonders with the chicks.'

'Is that a promise or a threat?' He twirled a lock of hair as if it was getting too straight.

'Cross my heart, handsome.'

He licked his teeth. 'Why don't we cut the crap and go inside. My hair can't take much more of this drizzle.'

'You call this drizzle. You can't be Swedish.'

'On the contrary. So what do you say?'

'OK. You're the first to talk to me tonight, and you'll be the first to have me, I guess.'

DiLeva giggled.

We held hands and rushed through the circle of dancing human frogs. They were croaking, 'Små grodorna, små grodorna är lustiga att se.'

Now the tough part: remembering sex. Is there anything harder in the world? Except for doing it in a bathtub?

The curly-head was a bloke. Now I remember. I'm quite positive. I have a vague image of holding something not quite hard in my hand. Squeezing it didn't do the trick. Curly-head pinched me, and giggled.

'Glad you're happy.'

'Thanks. Now if you will spread your legs a wee bit more. That's it. Good brilliant heavenly.'

'Don't mention it. Pleasure is all mine.'

I lost track of time. I'm quite sure we wrapped it up at some point. I broke into a sweat. Yes, that's a symptom. Definitely done it. I did my part. Curly-head did his.

We went out into the rain and held hands with the rest of the frogs circling around the hay-goat with a red ribbon. I croaked, 'Små grodorna, små grodorna är lustiga att se.'

BAYERN, BAYERN

It's football time in Munich. Again. Same thing every autumn, packs of football fans rush by me and disappear into local bars, howling, 'Bayern Bayern', and I don't know if the team won or lost, if they're keyed up for victory or disappointed after a lost game. I can't locate where the crowd is coming from. The arena's not that close to this part of the city. I feel nuts. Every face in the crowd is like an echo, or perhaps a doppelganger of some of my customers, people I've been pleasuring for ten years now.

The closest hooligan-free bar sucks me in and even though I never drink booze, today I feel like getting drunk. I've been to this bar before with a couple of girls. They call it Drei Drei Drei (Three Three Three). It has three fat, but clean, bartenders, and you have to order at least three seidels of beer before they crack a smile. Everything costs three times as much as in any other decent place. They say the beer's great, but all I've ever had is Schweppes, bitter soda.

The place is small and vibrates with deep male voices. The owners have provided only a small TV, yet every man gazes at the screen. The only man who isn't broken and bald moves a little to the left to make an opening at the bar for me. He sticks out from the usual crowd, his skin is black, he wears a light grey suit and smells like the fresh Aqua de Gio, though his sweat gives it an extra twist. His fist-long beard has beautifully hanging curls. His hair is bushy, yet his arms seem shaven. I edge closer. He says to the bartender, 'Another one.' The double-chinned man puts a glass of bright red fluid in front of me.

'I call it the Red Sea,' the black man says and takes a long slow sip, hardly changing the level in the glass. I can tell he is at least forty; there are white hairs in his beard and wrinkles on his forehead and around his mouth. He must have been smiling a lot in his life.

'I guess you like to be called Moses.'

'Joyce goes just fine.'

'May I call you James?'

'Joyce O'Hara.'

'All right then, Joyce.' I switch to English and his eyes brighten. 'A bloody Irish, ha." I say. "I thought your German was funny.' At that moment I don't feel like turning down the drink, so I take a sip and suddenly feel as if I am in another world. It's cranberry juice. I try to keep my face straight and I ask, 'You're having your period or what?'

He smiles. He has a small slot between his big front teeth, like my first lover, Aziz. I shudder at the thought of him but shake it off like a dog shakes off water. I breathe deep to relax. I figure Joyce is lying about his name, but I like the spiel. If he wants for a moment to be someone else, that's fine, I'm used to it. I say, 'Irish, I like that. Been here a while, mate?'

'Couple of years. I'm with Bayern.'

'Say no more. Playing?'

He reacts to the irony by slightly biting his lip, and then he says, 'Coaching.'

'Even worse. So the football-god brought you here?'

'Not really. It was love. A woman.'

'Ha, you must be an awful coach.'

'You can say that again. Or not really, I mean Bayern is a big team, after all. But then you're right, marriage and football zeal, it's tough, like having two mistresses you can't live without. Anyway, my wife split the other year and the rest is, well you've heard this story before, right?' He turns back to face the bartender who's wiping clean a big, ceramic seidel and sneering at him. He mutters, 'I'm boring you,' and tips his head forward.

I sit beside him and pull my glass close to my cleavage. I can tell he has caught the move out of the corner of his eye and is fighting not to stare. He starts to fidget with a coin. I say, 'On the contrary, a pitch-black Irishman sipping at a glass of cranberry juice, in Germany, of all places. I can swallow that, but to pose as the Bayern coach, now that's sacrilegious. I live here, dammit. The man who leads the Reds to victory nowadays is called Ottmar Hitzfeld, and he looks like Swiss cheese.'

He laughs. It's as if he wanted to test me with that bizarre picture of himself. I ask, 'So really, where are you from?'

'Ireland. Honest to God. I live there. I'm originally Nigerian, but I've lived half my life with the Irish. My mother married one back in the eighties.'

'So you weren't totally bullshitting me?'

'No. But my name's not Joyce, it's Jonah.'

'What brings you to Munich, Jonah?'

'I'm here to talk to some journalists and writers about a project we're starting.'

'No kidding, you a writer?'

'Goodness, no. I'm just a supporter of this organization called PEN. Ever heard of it?'

I wave my head.

'It's like an international support group for writers under persecution by their governments. We fight for freedom of speech and press, you know, basically help people out. The president is a Nigerian author and that's how I got into it, it's somewhat personal for me, but I'm really just a small businessman. I sell organic food in the UK.'

'So you're the good guy, helping people out even when you don't get filthy rich. Reminds me of my . . . ah never mind.'

'What?'

'Nothing. You're very original. You stand out, like in this bar.'

He turns around and takes a look at the other guests. There is one bloke in the steamy atmosphere who might be a Turk, but he has bleached blonde hair. Jonah says, 'I never thought of myself as original. You seem to care for that.'

'Not really, but it can come in handy at times. A good story's what everyone wants. A year ago a German immigration judge declined a Somali woman her residence permit, because her story was full of clichés.'

'You're kidding? What did she say?'

'Lots of murder, someone burnt down her house, then rape, you know, the usual bitter clichés of war. The damn judge said he'd heard that story before.'

'That's horrible. How do you know all this? Are you a lawyer or something?'

I laugh so much it feels as if my lips are cracking. 'Not really. Though I have a special bond to law and law-people.' I haven't laughed like this in years. I feel vulnerable, open, but also great. I wouldn't mind laughing more. My God, have I come so far in my life that I can say, Once upon a time I laughed? 'This woman, she's a hooker now, just four blocks from here, in the so-called crimson belt of the city.'

'Really, where's that?'

'Ah, you're interested already. It's an imaginary ring that cuts through the city, neither the centre nor suburbia. That's where the big brothels are, stuff like that.'

Jonah drops the coin, but doesn't bend down to get it. He blushes. 'Are you . . . ?'

I wipe the sweat breaking from my eyebrow thinking, Here we go again, you can't hide, you're a 101 prostitute; it's in your blood now, you're a stereotype now, like computer geeks, cops, mad scientists, or fair ladies. I say, 'I have to make a phone call.' The bartender directs me with his hitching thumb. I go there and pretend I'm talking to someone for ten minutes.

Back at the bar, I grab my glass, which the Nigerian has moved closer to his, and without giving it much thought, drink it all. I laugh again. 'Cranberry juice, I hear that's good for bladder infections.'

He laughs and I can see his big molars. I love that. He finishes up his juice and says, 'So, what's your story? You can start with a name. A false one will do.'

I never use a false name. I want there to be a little piece of me in every pretending. I say crisply, 'Fatima.'

His eyes bulge and both his hands glide down to his knees.

'I'd never guess you're Middle Eastern.'

'Don't worry. I won't blow you up.'

'I'd take you for a regular German girl.'

'Bosnian.'

'Ha, I see. You got me there. Bosnia, you say? I imagined you'd be more like, I don't know, the Turks.'

I say nothing. He goes on, 'I heard Germany's sending you all back.'

'I guess I had an original story to give and got to stay.'

He looks like a kid staring at sweets behind a thick window. 'Which is?'

'Lost love,' I say, trying to laugh at myself, but failing. I am glad that at least he can laugh at me. 'I'm like my father. He left his whole family in Western Bosnia to move in with Mum in this mountain town. He rebelled against the old tradition that a man should stay where he is and bring a wife home. Lucky that Mum was rich.'

He gives me that say-no-more-I-know-what-you-mean look.

I hiss, 'Hey, he wasn't like that. He loved her.'

'I'm sure.'

'Screw that tone!'

He bends his head down then looks up again with those puppy eyes and a sad expression. I bite my thumbnail a little, then take hold of the empty glass just to remove the finger from my mouth. I laugh.

'What is it?'

'It's just so funny. I can almost see Mum right now, the way she moved like old Bosnian noble people, flaunting all the exclusive-edition books they bought for me. They put a lot into my education. I guess I'd be something of a disappointment to them now.'

Jonah says nothing for a while then, 'I assume your parents are dead. I'm sorry.'

I feel off guard. Why am I talking about my parents?

'You loved them a lot, didn't you?'

'Yes, but then, I don't know, really. My father was always working, and Mum, she always wanted us to sit close to each other, safe and preened, no matter what. Well yes, I did love them a lot. I've just put all that behind me.'

Jonah snaps his fingers at the sulky bartender and gets another round of juice. I take a sip and shudder. When I first saw Jonah, I thought to take him home with me, but now that he has dug up some old memories of mine, I don't know. I don't really feel like having ordinary sex, none of that cosy making-love. I don't feel like extraordinary sex either. I don't feel like anything but walking by the Isar and feeding the swans.

Jonah is silent as a fish. I scan him from top to toe and drink up the bitter beverage. I kiss my fingertips and touch the rim of his glass, saying, 'Well, I doubt you can afford anything else. Don't get yourself drowned.' I leave the bar, wondering if he's watching me as I exit the building.

I flow up the street with the river of people who are crying, 'Bayern Bayern.'

Later in the evening, I sit on the toilet, muttering, 'That damn cranberry juice.' I think I might have some slight infection after all. Or perhaps I am just nervous. I've had this problem for years now. It's not an easy thing to deal with in my profession. Every day's different. Every task demands the best performance. I try not to lie down and simply let myself be screwed in a passive way. That doesn't make a man come back. Sometimes I eat a lot of chocolate to get constipation. Ah, no one wants to hear such things.

The next morning, to cap it all off, I have this unexplained butterflies-in-the-belly feeling and I don't like it. I don't like it at all. Is my body trying to tell me I have a crush on the Nigerian already? Why did I go away from him so quickly, and with that kind of remark? Because I feared he'd wake up the next morning and toss me some money? Have I started to shun men I like?

Butterflies keep multiplying so I decide to put myself and my destiny to a test. In the evening, I will go to the same Drei Drei Drei bar, hoping to find that Nigerian fighter for the maladjusted writers. The odds are against me, no doubt, but then maybe I made a great impression. If he isn't there, then fate decided it that way, but if he is, then I'll thank God and start thinking about how to pursue this familiar but uncanny feeling for a man.

I try on every dress I have, every pair of stockings and shoes. I decide what make-up and what eau de toilette go with what garments. In the end I shove everything back into my wardrobe and put on black trousers, a purple jumper that Mary knitted for me as thanks for that rich customer I gave her, and finally a long winter jacket I got from the Red Cross back in Bosnia, which I keep as a memento.

I paint my face quite sloppily, and rush out. The air is so cold I can hardly open my eyes. Instead, I fumble my way to the S-Bahn stop. It takes almost an hour to get downtown. There's an accident close to the city centre. The streetcar stops at one point, close to the river Isar. I take this as a sign and before I go to the bar, I walk down to the Isar to wash off my make-up. There is a crust of ice over the surface close to the banks. In the middle, the stream is still free. A frozen swan floats by.

The bar door is like a stone slab. My frozen arm feels like shattering as I both push and pull because the door won't open either way. I pant and then push hard. It opens and my eyes become misty as Max's glasses do when he enters my warm room on a cold day.

I squint. Jonah's not there, of course. I almost wave my hand at the sky thinking, You just don't give me a break, do you? I feel an instant remorse for my thoughts, as if some sense of spirituality tells me I can't hurry the Boss in doing what he feels is right for me. I got this from mekteb, an extra-curricular, weekend religious education I attended for five years. I liked going there with other girls and boys, before imam Atif became more and more ill. My parents didn't force me. They weren't particularly religious. Mum only followed the other women to the mosque during Ramadan. Father's religious practice boiled down to occasionally crying out, 'My God,' 'Inshallah,' and 'Goddamn,' like the bulk of the new Communists did out of old habit. Only my parents never made good Communists either.

I survey the bar once again to make sure Jonah isn't inside, then turn back to the door.

'Fatima?' My name rings nicely with that strange accent. I want everything around me to freeze for a moment so I can take a couple more cold breaths, but no such luck, I have to turn round and face him. Water is dropping from his fingers and he dries them against his baggy trousers. He wears a white jumper like the ones golfers wear. I read from his rapidly opening and closing lids that he's both surprised to see me and that he's been here for a while, perhaps ever since I first left him, hoping I'd come back. Obviously, he hasn't been drinking anything strong, yet his hands tremble and his lips have become thinner and paler.

I walk over to Jonah, determined not to ponder serendipity, coincidence, or fate. I fear that any answers, true or false, would ruin everything. I just let everything be as it is for the moment.

I take his extra-large hand into my extra-small one, and lead him outside into the traffic buzz, kiss him right there in the street for everyone to see, and then take him home. I lead him in without turning on the lights. That way he won't get a sense of the place.

At first, I fuck the Nigerian fast, just to break the already thawing ice, and then let him fall asleep. I put on a negligee and fall asleep myself. My dreams set me on fire and I wake, ready to conquer my lover, this time thoroughly. I suck him dry of all his riches, like a real empress. Only I have no country to back me up, no imperial power behind me.

His sighs rustle like autumn leaves. His black skin is hairless and his palms gentle. I contract. He twitches and moans. I'm wet inside out. I don't call his name. I sit on him, light as my warm silhouette on the wall opposite the window lit up by crescent moons. He twitches, one two three times, and his head falls back on the pillow. I wait until he grows limp and then I pull myself from his slack penis and leave it drenched in my smell. A trickle of blood runs down my thigh, lukewarm and quick, but it stops just above my knee and curdles. I don't feel pain.

My negligee vibrates in the draught when I go out of the bedroom and into the kitchen. I take a notebook and a pencil. It's so dark I can't tell the pages from the cool air. It doesn't matter. I know they are blank. Then, as if the pen forces me, I write down a name, Aziz. I press the tip against the paper. It sinks deep and sticks in this self-made hole. The ink seeps out and wets the paper and I walk into the loo, throw the pen into the toilet, but then take it out immediately and put it in between the blank sheets. The paper sucks it dry. I go back to the kitchen and put it in the large tea jar I got from a Japanese customer a few years ago.

I go back to Jonah, turn the paper lamp on, and pull the blanket off him. With hungry eyes, I divide him into parts, deciding on what bits and pieces are good for what dish. Some bits and pieces tingle the tip of the tongue, some are best when they fill the whole mouth, some when they only touch the back of the throat or the hard cavity.

I touch his circumcised penis. For a big bloke like him, his testicles are unusually small. An old fear drums in my head. I lift up his balls, check and double-check everything. It's my old anxiety kicking in. Even so many years after Aziz and I separated, whenever I unbutton someone's trousers, my hands shake for fear to discover someone else with the same secret. I slow everything down: slowly touching, slowly feeling, slowly smelling, and slowly listening to the person's breathing. Judge Max told me that this quality of mine fascinated him, my constant anxiety. Most girls know what they have to do and do it mechanically, to get over and done with it. I still fear what's going to happen, every single time fear overtakes me and it shows even when my hands are in control. That excites people.

There's nothing wrong with Jonah. I look at his bearded face. He looks like this bust of the Spartan king Leonidas that I saw in the office of Professor Stier a year ago. It was made of dirty white plaster. Professor made a bed of books on the carpeted floor, tied me to the column that held the bust of Leonidas and took me from behind. I stared at the engraved name as Professor kept impersonating a lion.

I crawl back next to my lover, take his hand, and slip it between my legs. He wakes up. He won't let me suck him. Instead, he wants to please only me now. He kisses me from head to foot, licking me exhausted. Then, when I'm slowly vibrating like the heavy sound that lingers both inside and outside the brass shell of a tube, when I no longer can open my eyes for fear he'll disappear, he enters me and I climax, one two ... then relax.

Hoping thought can stream from my head to his, I think, Marry me, Jonah. Make me legitimate in the eyes of the people, any people. Take me away from here. I kind of regret thinking the last part. I love Munich, but I once loved Aziz and still I left him.

A couple of nights later, I wave to my Nigerian Leonidas as he drags his feet up the stairs to a green plane bound for Ireland. In my other hand I clutch his business card with a number jotted on the back. The secret number. I gave him a number too.

He calls the following morning, before even Munich traffic has woken up. I try to make myself talk because I'm absolutely stunned. He actually called. As with my first date, I have nothing to say for fear he will find me boring, but I can't hold his hand and glance at him either. I sit in silence; the clock's ticktock is like a bell.

'Fatima.'

God, I love the way my name breaks in that Irish accent.

'Jonah.'

'I think I'm going to apply for the Bayern coach position.'

I laugh. 'I can be your secretary then.'

'You tease. I can't stop thinking about you.'

I want to say the same but keep gulping saliva.

'Can you come to Ireland?'

Damn, now I definitely don't know what to say.

'Fatima, are you still there?'

Oh, I'm still here, but I wish I was on a plane to Dublin. 'Right here. You see . . . oh my God. All right,' I say, in the same tone of voice I once used to deliver my oral exams back in school. 'I'm an illegal immigrant, Jonah. Unless you can find some tough sailor with an old rusty boat to smuggle me over there, chances are I'll never see U2 playing at home.'

Now he doesn't know how to respond.

'Besides, you know what I am, don't pretend you don't.'

'I know, I know, I've been thinking about it ever since I met you, but I don't think I care. I want you beside me.'

I feel weak and move to lie on the floor. 'I like you too, Jonah, and I don't care what you do for a living either.'

He laughs nervously. 'Is there any way you could come round?'

'I told you. They say Europe is losing its borders, but that doesn't mean you don't get checked when you cross these non-existing walls.'

'All right. I'll see what I can do. You don't happen to be an exiled writer or something, because then I could ask the PEN to help you out.'

At that moment a vision opens up before me as if it were projected on an old, rotting screen. The romantic flick type of vision. My God, could this for one second be an opportunity. A writer, does that include a wannabe journalist? I don't dare ask. Instead, as the reel carrying my alternate future starts tangling in the projector and begins to melt from the heat of the machine, I say, 'No, not a writer. But maybe I should give it a try. Write a memoir or some such thing.'

'Maybe, Fatima. Can you? You'd have to prove yourself. These people are rather posh. They only support the best. Preferably political writers.'

I say, as if it mattered, 'No romance?'

'I don't know. I can ask.'

'Stop it now.'

'What?'

'Stop messing with my head. Stop blowing Irish fantasies into my head. Can you come here? Can you smuggle me out? Can you come like a damn superhero riding on a whale to fetch me by the Isar bank? I didn't think so. It was really nice meeting you, Jonah.'

I hang up, then think, my God what have I done? Why can't I be nicer? I love fantasies, but I just hate being in them, I can't do it or I'll end up in a lunatic asylum, if they still keep such places. Now that'd be real-life solution: feign I'm crazy.

For months, Jonah does not call. I'm still having glimpses of him. One night, I imagine him in the strange shape of one Siamese twin, the other half being my old love, Aziz. Jonah to the right, Aziz to the left. They are attached at the hips and shoulders, with only one free arm each. I shake my head to separate them or remove that horrible image completely from my head. Jonah fades away, but not Aziz. The mind forgets things easily, but my whole goddamn body remembers my lovers. It's like that osmosis experiment I did in the sixth grade with peas and lukewarm water. The two are completely different but when they meet, the small thing sucks the huge one into itself and then they grow together into something else.

GUSUL

Emina is working, but her work, the autistic boy Stig, is scuttling from gravestone to gravestone around Stockholm's Katarina Church, knocking over aluminium vases and yellow flowers, his long blonde hair wet and glued to his face. He sings the latest Swedish hit that bombed at the Eurovision Song Contest, 'I wanna be like a star like a hero, love will survive.'

The ghosts of Sweden past that sit on the mossy and cobbled Church grounds seem kind and cheerful to Emina. They do not look at her with derision. They do not mind that she is looking straight through them as if they did not grace her with their presence. The grave of Erik the smithy is well fenced, so that Ivar the baker and Irma the milkmaid do not enter his space like they used to do in the times when the city customs still meant more than the invisible barrier between the rich and the filthy rich.

Emina rests her eyes on the family grave of Gottfried the watchmaker and finishes her turkey sandwich. Her mother's old blue cardigan makes her look a decade older than her thirty-five. Her face is dry. She has forgotten again to apply the face butter from the Body Shop.

Stig loves the churchyard, where ghosts are so old they have few relatives to bother them with odourless flowers. Yet, there are always a few nostalgic descendants who honour the dead they found in some old record book. Now there is a middle-aged couple, both with the same crewcut and green rubber boots, working on a flower arrangement. They scowl at Stig as he does his Spider Man impersonation in front of them.

'Stick härifrån, din lilla snorunge,' the man hisses.

Emina stands up as if pricked in her heels, walks by the green-fingered couple and catches Stig when he jumps between two granite gravestones. He laughs into her left ear and kisses her on the temple. She hates calming him down, especially when he claims the open space as if there's no such thing as social borders. His autism usually keeps him silent and cornered in his classroom.

Emina puts Stig down. 'Go and finish your McChicken. You have to be back home in half an hour.' She keeps her back turned to the couple who are still muttering, 'Låta pojken hoppa runt kyrkogår'n.'

'Så oförskämt.'

Stig scratches his ears under the soaked hair. 'I want to see your mum, the superhero.'

'The Superhero?'

'Yes, she's the Rogue.'

'What's the Rogue?'

'Not what, who. She's the powerful X-Man who steals other mutants' powers. She has black and white hair. Like your mum.'

Emina pulls him into her arms, sweeps aside the hair from his face, and says. 'Tell you what, she is the Rogue, but you mustn't tell anyone. She's old now and has lost her powers.'

'Cool. Is that why she doesn't speak?'

Emina folds up as if someone cut her sinews, and surge of memory makes her feel irresponsible, unfocused on the boy. Stig straddles her and peers into her pupils as if his eyes were a doctor's light. He seems to be in charge, the grown-up as well as being carefree and happy.

She makes herself laugh and says, 'She doesn't speak because she's lost someone, a fellow hero.'

'Cool.'

'Yes. Very cool. If you talk to her, maybe she'll speak with you.'

Stig cups his hands in front of his mouth and giggles. 'Good goody good. When?'

'Maybe on Sunday. Your mother can drop you off after church.'

'Don't like it. The preacher speaks strange.'

Emina wants to ask him why he dislikes the priest, but then she remembers what his parents told her at the job interview. Stig's autism means he cannot understand general nouns, concepts, abstractions. He can't see how murder and jealousy are both sins, how Jesus can be both a man and a God. Emina once told him that maybe Jesus the man is the secret identity of Jesus the God, like Clark Kent and Superman. Stig said, 'Cool.'

Emina lies down and rests her head on the cobbles. Stig tears away to fetch the rest of his cold burger.

Emina walks into her flat like she would step on a bus, as if to get somewhere. The damp walls smell of dogs even though it's been over a year since the old tenants moved out. She walks into the bathroom, washes her hands with peach soap, and smells her fingertips.

In the bedroom, her mother's body seems to have grown roots into her bed. The smell of urine does not prevent Emina from smiling. She kisses her mother on the cheek. 'Mum, do you need to go to the toilet?'

The woman nods.

Emina lifts her up as if she's pulling a plant, gently, because she must place her back there once she has changed the soiled sheets.

The seventy-two-year-old woman coughs. Coughing, panting and snoring are the only sounds she uses to communicate, and Emina can distinguish nine moods of her mother's mind from them. She changes the sheets, remembering how, four years earlier, she stopped hanging white sheets in her backyard for fear they could be shot at like all the white flags during the Balkan war.

When her mother lies down again and starts snoring, Emina thinks she is just pretending to be asleep in order to make Emina feel better, but the snoring is real, loud, and, Emina says, I love your snoring.

No reaction.

Emina laughs, takes up a picture of her father wearing a white ahmedija on his head, typical for a Bosnian imam. She closes her eyes. The ahmedija falls on the ground outside a small stone mosque with a blue tin roof. Some soil covers it as thousands of feet pass by pass by pass by. Grass grows out, and weeds, the inedible things. Around her, there is more green now. Evergreen woods of Southern Sweden, and the meadows between them, and a grey motorway spruced with colourful cars. Lots of red cars. Volvos and Saabs, and Volkswagens.

Emina opens her eyes and says, without turning to her mother, 'When I was a little girl you could never shut up.'

She caresses the picture with the cleaning cloth. 'Father was the imam, but you, you wrote his sermons. By Thursday night, you had his Friday jumah speech ready. You read it to us in a candle-lit kitchen, and we listened and sometimes said, Do it again, just to enjoy your voice.'

She looks at the thin, aubergine-coloured lips opening and closing, and she tries to remember the voice, but she can only recall images, as if she has been deaf all her life. She swallows spit three times, and says, 'Remember the night our ferry arrived at Ystad, where we spent our first week in that huge hangar with some two hundred chatting yelling farting refugees? The officers at the refugee centre questioned us: How much money are you carrying? Do you have relatives here? How long do you plan on staying?' She pauses. 'You just kept silent.'

The frame slips from her hand and falls to the floor. Emina

glances at her mother, but she doesn't seem to have heard anything. Emina picks up the frame, kisses the black and white, clean-shaven face, and puts it amid other pictures of herself as a baby, as a girl with braids, as a young woman with loads of emotions and equations in her mind, and as a genderless refugee outside a corroded bus holding the hand of a mute mother.

'Emina, my feet are cold,' her mother says.

Emina keeps wiping the pictures. Then, as if the message was garbled and her brain took a while to decipher it, she stops, looking at the photo of her mother's wrinkle-less face as if it was that young woman who spoke to her. She turns around.

The second time the thin voice is higher, 'Emina, my feet are cold.'

Emina straddles the narrow bed, takes her mother by the calves, and presses the soles of her feet against her warm stomach. The tangled, purple veins seem to be glued onto the cellophane skin of the feet, rather than growing like weed underneath. Emina rubs her calves and the skin creases, and the veins change patterns. She opens her mouth to say something, but doesn't, for fear there is some limit to the number of words that can be said right there and then.

The mother smiles, and says, 'I'd like some plum pie.'

'Plum pie?'

She nods.

Emina stands up, tucks the moist feet under the blanket, and gives her mother some water. The woman swallows one gulp.

'I'll go and make you some pie.' But she can't move. She kisses her mother on the lips and then gives her more water. She caresses her long grey hair, and the single lime-white lock. She thinks, the Rogue, huh.

In the kitchen, which is just outside the bedroom, Emina produces a bowl of dark plums, sugar, flour, oil, and a round earthenware dish as if everything was already right there ready at hand, just waiting for the wish to be uttered. Plum pie is the black sheep among all the different Bosnian pies, more like plum jam with cream and no dough.

Emina pours oil into the dish, and says, 'Mother, you know Stig. He said you looked like some super woman from his comic books, who absorbs other people's powers.' She cracks open the plums, pulls out the stones with her teeth, spits the stones into the kitchen sink, and lays plum-halves in circles in the dish. 'I told him you're the one, but he must keep it hush hush.'

She pinches some sugar and throws it on the plums. Then she does the same with flour, and finally pours cream until the plums swim in it.

Ten minutes in the hot oven, the plums are soft and she opens the oven but leaves the dish inside for five more minutes, and then she puts it on the windowsill and opens the window just a crack. She stands at door to the bedroom and watches her mother's nose wiggle. The woman tries to say something, the tip of her tongue pressing the back of her teeth. 'L . . . l . . . la.'

As if the old body is already dead and her mother's soul is passing over the thin and sharp Sirat bridge towards the open gates of Jannat al-Adn, Emina grabs her face and presses her lips against her mother's.

When she releases her, her mother says, 'La-ilaha-ilallah, Muhammedun Resulullah.'

Emina cries, 'No, not now, please, not the shahada.'

Her mother now raises her voice and repeats, 'La-ilaha-ilallah, Muhammedun Resulullah.'

The second testimony of faith pushes Emina backwards, like a hand, and she scowls and breathes hard through her nose and she looks up at the clock and then through the window. There is a couple on a balcony of the building just opposite theirs. They are laughing and drinking coffee from big cups, and the woman pours more into her man's cup, and she tosses her hair back and puts her hands under her breasts as if weighing them, and he nods and laughs, and Emina feels like slapping them but she cannot stop watching them while her mother keeps chanting the shahada, slower and slower, and Emina presses her fingers into her eyes and then turns to see that her mother's eyes are closed and she has stopped repeating the phrase, but her chest is still rising and falling, Emina puts her head on her mother's left breast and prays, and she watches the light grow stronger on the barely visible patterns of the wallpapers, and she continues to pray long after her mother has stopped breathing.

Later, she cannot tell how much later, Emina wipes the few tears and struggles not to cry. She sits on the bedside, her back turned to her mother. Then she slips under her quilt and covers herself up to her nose, the way she did when she was a kid, before she started school and stopped fearing the shadows of the quince tree under the twin moons.

Emina stands in the hall, watching the telephone as if waiting to hear it speak for her. She lifts up the receiver and pushes it under her black hair as under a hat and punches the numbers with her knuckles.

'This is Seima.'

'Salaam-u-alaykum. May I speak with imam Atif?'

'Atif.'

'Salaam-u-alaykum. This is Emina Begović.'

'Alaykum-u-salaam.'

'My mother has died.'

'I'm sorry for your loss. She was a pious woman, she has moved on to a better world.'

'I haven't cried.'

'Good. The tears of the beloved ones burn the soul of the deceased.'

Silence.

'Emina, have you called the medics, the morgue, anyone?'

'No.'

He breathes out like a smoker. 'All right. Then I'll do it for you.'

Emina presses the receiver harder against her ear. 'Please let me wash her. Tuck her in one last time.'

'Pull yourself together. This is most unusual. It's a ritual. We have women trained for that.'

'Please, I need to do it. I must.'

'Would you even know?'

'I've seen my parents gusul dozens of bodies. I could wash my mother with my eyes closed. I'll sweep her into a ćefin.'

'Are you sure?'

'Yes.'

'Do what you must. I'll arrange for a coffin.'

'Coffin? Why coffin?'

'Emina, remember where you are. The Swedish law prescribes a coffin.'

'Thank you.'

Emina watches the small daisy flowers on the wallpaper. Next she becomes conscious of her body, she finds herself carrying the plum pie as if to an angry queen who ordered it long time ago but never received it. She places it under her mother's nose and waits. The sweet smell fails to tease her back to life.

Another time lag. Another gap in the mind.

Now she is neatly folding her mother's quilt, a patchwork of all colours on earth. There is a smell. Unfamiliar. She inhales it, slowly, as if not to hurt the air.

She leans over the naked feet and unbuttons the pyjamas, splays them open like a dogeared book. When she pulls out the pillow, her mother's mouth opens and the air remaining in her lungs blows out over Emina's right ear with the ease of the word 'La,' the negative, the negation before the affirmation.

Emina tears a white towel with her teeth. She dips each of the five pieces into a bowl of lukewarm water, squeezes out the water and dabs the body. The dark veins branch out from the ankles like the foot of an uprooted tree.

Emina can still smell the plums.

She washes the soles first, washes off her own sweat that rubbed off when she warmed the feet, then she moves the wet cloth up her mother's slender thighs up to the vagina. Next she cleans the scar from the Caesarean, and she recoils as if she's seen it for the first time, thinking, I've forgotten they cut me out of you.

She almost skips the breasts, which look uncannily young, and small, as if they've never fed a baby, or been kneaded by a man, and then moves up to the chin, with three long hairs, which her mother never let her pull out. Then she moves aside, over the shoulder and the twin scars from the vaccine, down to the indigo hand, which she strokes and presses against the bed before she pulls off the ring. Then she washes the ears, and takes time whispering, 'Eudubillahi mina shaytan irrajeem. Bismillahi-rrahmani-rrahim. Ya-Seen. Wal-Qur'anil hakeem . . .' When she rolls her mother onto her side to tighten a white ćefin around her the way mothers wrap babies so their bodies will grow straight, she thinks she can hear her collarbone cracking. She places her mother's thin braids over her breasts and then rests her own head on the edge of the bed.

The phone rings.

Emina picks up the receiver.

Atif says, 'Emina, I've notified the authorities. Someone will come to take her to the morgue.'

'I'm done. Mother looks like she did on hajj, twenty years ago.'

'Listen to me, this isn't Bosnia. We can't bury her today. I'll speed things up, but it'll take at least three days.'

Emina hangs up.

She takes the plum pie and half a loaf of hard, whole-wheat bread, and goes out the front door and sits down on the staircase. The buzzing bulbs colour the plums yellow-green, like toxic waste. She digs out the soft heart of the loaf, puts it into her pockets, chops off pieces of the crust, and scoops up plums. She does not chew. She gulps and gulps until the food sinks down her throat. She takes another bite, and one more before swallowing the first.

Two men in yellow vests walk into the building with a stretcher. A man that looks like a clean-shaven albino bear, and with no expression on his face asks, 'Where?'

Emina swallows and opens her mouth as if to say something, but she only points with her whole hand at the door. The man with thick glasses says, My condolences and gives her a paper to sign, and she draws an X and goes on choking on the plums and the bread until she hears the ambulance drive off.

Stig jumps from gravestone to gravestone in the Muslim section of Skogskyrkogården. Most stones have a crescent and a star carved close to the top, a name or names underneath. A few even have a small white bird perched on the last letter of the surname. Emina stares at a group of graves so close to each other as if the people in them were relatives. But, Ahmed the Egyptian, Zuleyha the Pakistani, Osman the Albanian, Safiya the Malay, and Ibrahim the Somali don't say much to each other. They speak to Emina, in their native tongues. A small-time town of Babel. Emina imagines they are gesticulating to help her understand their afterlife troubles.

Her mother is still silent.

Stig shouts to Emina, 'Look at this.' She lifts her eyes from the mound marked with her mother's name. Stig jumps off Zülfikar the Turk's marble gravestone, bends his legs and spreads his arms as if he is going to hug her. He presses his palms with his two middle fingers, to release the spider-web, and yells, 'Pfzzzz, pfzzzz.' He trips and falls flat on his stomach, and a second later he's up again. He pulls up his Spidey-suit, and points at his skinny torso. 'See, no injuries.'

WALKING ON ROOFS

My name is Niels Bohr. I was born in 1885, on a cold night, and I fell in love with heat. I liked pressing my fingertips to warm windowpanes, my wife's lips, lake pebbles outside my cabin, invisible grains of dust that shine up in the air.

Now I like to walk on roofs. When I first started in 1945, I was light as a candle flame. Unbearably light. I moved with ease of a sparrow with an olive leaf in its beak. I had the leg power of a stork that brings children to happy parents, and the mind of a raven. Powerful enough to play with atoms.

It is 2011 and I'm old now. Too old to be jumping from rooftop to rooftop in this Japanese village. Too old and too scared to go down to earth.

My fingers hurt when I lift a few decayed tiles and peer into the attic. Streetlight stirs dust. I don't go in. I don't sleep in other people's houses any longer. I snug up to smokeless chimneys on warm nights, or cringe close to the weathercocks.

I take no pleasure in watching nighttime tragedies and comedies of existence. I'm not a voyeur. I fall in love every night, at dusk and dawn, with beautiful mothers and fathers, sons and daughters, solitary streetwalkers, cats and mongrels, rats which never sleep, moths tangled in gossamer staring at candles in the windows.

Tonight, March 12, my one-hundred-and-twenty-five year-old feet hurt against the fragile roofs of this new village. It feels like it was yesterday I scurried the flat tops of New York.

The tiles are like glass dust.

I lie down on my stomach, my head hanging over the roof edge. The light in the room underneath is weak. A boy and a girl, twins, are watching a broken TV screen. I cannot hear sounds, but they may be talking. The girl's stiff fingers barely touch her brother's crew-cut hair. To his left there is a mask of a Samurai.

I tilt my head back and forth, trying to see who else is in the house. A dark-haired woman leans on the kitchen doorframe, smiling coyly at the bulky man doing yoga on the floor. Her heel is high up in the air. His four fingertips touch the tips of her toes, lifting them up from the floor linoleum, her thumb the only part of her delicate foot still pressed against the floor, as if he is trying to help her do a pirouette. They are stuck in that intimate gesture. There is no further movement. She is not a ticklish subject to his tickling experiment with her sole.

I hitch myself up and look over the village. Cats and mongrels, rats and nightingales, yes, they're all there. But they are all too silent, too sleepy, too lazy, crouched close to backyard fences and neatly parked cars. I must have gone deaf. I hear no sounds, not even the desert wind. The air is uncannily calm. The trees are petrified.

I spy through more windows. In the smallest house, seven children sit in a circle around a huge bowl of cornbread crumbled and drenched in milk. A father sits hunched in a corner crying, his palms pressed against his eyeballs. The mother is probably in the kitchen.

Across the street, a man and a woman are stuck in the missionary position, their faces distorted with the painful pleasures.

In the largest house with three windows, a boy yells at his brother, who holds his Iron Man toy high in the air, threatening to break its left leg. In the third room their grandma is kissing a picture of a handsome moustachioed man in a turban.

For the first time I jump down on the ground. The asphalt is cold. Temperature drops like Newton's infamous apple. I never thought of that, does the gravity affect temperature? How about human warmth?

I walk the empty streets like a straggler. Water runs down the street and splashes at my toes like small rocks. At the edge of the town, the sun is coming up patiently. Still, it's the break of the day. This light is intense, immaculate, warm. The cloud at the horizon does not shield me from the dawn. I put my hands in the air as if to press my fingertips against the hot dusty wind. I glimpse a wall of dark water.

WAR CURRENCY

Sex didn't help me out of the war in Bosnia. A matter of mis-judgement, naivety, bad luck, fate, take your pick.

On the snowy February 14, 1993, the tenth month of the war, my mother was wielding huge kitchen scissors, which chewed my hair as she struggled to cut the locks held steady between her fingers. The hair fell to the floor and I sobbed. I was nineteen.

Mum comforted me like a crooner without music. 'Don't cry. It'll grow back again. It's better this way. Easier to keep clean. Keeps the lice away.'

'I hate it.'

'You'll look at least four years younger.'

'I don't want to look younger.'

Mum kept struggling with the dull scissors, muttering, 'At least soldiers will keep their eyes off you.'

'Maybe I want them to see me.'

'I don't want to see you with a rifle.'

'You mean those. I'm thinking maybe a handsome Dutch officer will take me to the land far away and long ago. Like Lara.' My old girlfriend Lara was way luckier to hook up with that French UN officer, an old fellow, man enough to knock her up but take responsibility.

Mum hit me on the neck with the smooth part of the scissors.

'You're so fucking dull.'

She hit me again.

'All right, Mum, all right, knock it off.'

I looked at her trying to see the traces of the woman who, back in the 60s, had spread her legs to an old city slicker to cooapo her mountain village and freshly manured fields. She'd left her mucky footwear and ran barefoot to a small Sarajevo flat with a shiny wooden floor, straightened her back and ironed her clothes, her fat feet sweating in hard high-heel shoes as if they'd never experienced the comfort of rubber galoshes.

She ruffled my now-mowed hair, laughed, went to the kitchen, fetched the little broom crudely made of thin twigs, and brushed my shoulders. She said, 'Look at you. Now you're a little boy.'

I checked my hair in a little piece of broken mirror. I looked nothing like my late father. I'm blonde, my nose is perky and freckled, my lips sensual. Mum's friends used to stop us in the street, scan me and say with those peevish voices, 'You're the spitting image of your mother.' I hated the word 'spitting.' I'd wipe my hand across my eyes and my cheeks. That was before the war, when the only things we had to hate were petty things. I said, 'Come on. Damn ugly. Now no one will ever look at me again.' I went to my bedroom, but I could hear Mum saying softly, 'That's the whole point.'

The walls of my room were full of holes but well patched with cupboard doors, floor planks, linoleum, you name it. I pushed the piece of a flattened tin that covered a grenade hole and peered out just to see the same old street life. In the distance was a woman trying to take the short cut between two twenty-storey 'towers' on the way to the water and food supply at Merhamet. There was sixty percent chance she'd stay forever in the spot, her blood basking in the weak winter sun. I'd seen two guys betting as to who'd get to pass with their skin intact and who wouldn't. A shot hit her and she fell, plunging face forward into the asphalt.

I slipped into my jeans, which were torn, but now no longer

fashionable. I put on my father's white shirt with a dark stain around the collar. My dad's throat was slit by a flying piece of car shell outside his downtown office, but the piece of metal had been overheated and it'd scorched Dad's flesh. It had cauterized the wound with surgical precision. Some blood had come out after all. I zipped my jacket up to the chin to hide the shirt and a bracelet I'd made of dulled barbed wire and colourful threads. Then I heard what seemed like a distant knocking on the front door. I walked to the kitchen, saying, 'Must be Jasmina.'

Mum was sitting at the kitchen table, close to another big hole in the outer wall, which was covered with plastic shaking in the wind. The table's legs were half sawn-off and there was fumeless coffee in a small cup. She looked up from the table and sighed as I opened the door an inch and winked to Jasmina to wait there.

Mum muttered, 'Where are you going?'

'Out.'

'Can't you go down the street and see if the cistern's arrived yet?

'No.'

'Please, my hands are killing me.' She pointed to two ten-litre canisters and a broom handle.

'So we've got two now. Awesome.'

'Minka upstairs gave me one. There was still some oil in it, so you'll get extra-fat nail soup tonight. Come to think of it, no, we're out of nails, it'll be a bullet soup.'

'Whatever.'

'Look at you, so skinny. Nothing to fill those clothes.'

I grabbed the canisters and the broom handle. 'Knock it off, Mum. Fat is bad, even in war. I'm out of here.'

Mum finished her coffee and turned over the cup, pouring the resin out, and then examined the pattern it had left on the cup walls.

I struggled with the slippery canisters and my shirt came untucked and shone from beneath my jacket. She hollered,

'What's that you're wearing? You little . . . why are you wearing your father's shirt?

'Fuck you, Mum. I loved him too.'

She lifted her hand with the coffee cup still in it and was about to hurl it at me when she realized she only had the one cup, and she put it back with an affectionate look and without a word. I inched out as she slouched over the table whispering something to the cup. The canisters had a life of their own when I dashed out and nudged Jasmina on the shoulder. Her face looked like a pimple country. She had pretty much the same clothes as hundreds of others in the city, very warm stuff that had fallen from the sky by the dozen two months earlier. The door slammed but only bounced back and forth against the doorframe because the lock was broken. Dad didn't get a chance to fix it, and mother wouldn't let me do it either.

Outside our five-storey building that looks like a sieve, it was snowing, and the snowflakes, as big as a child's fists, were eddying in the sky as if this was their last chance to fall. We walked down the street and towards a place where, usually, a row of people waited with canisters to get their water ration from the cistern.

Jasmina said, 'Is that your father's shirt?'

I said nothing.

'How long has it been now?'

'Who counts?'

'The stains . . . you haven't —'

'Mum won't wash it.'

Jasmina nodded.

'I guess it's the only thing we agree about.'

Jasmina said, 'I still can't believe that arsehole said you were lucky there wasn't much blood. Bastard Blue Helmet.'

'No, he was our guy. He looked like he was with the Smurfs, blue uniform and all, but this was before the UN came. He even spoke English as if he'd just fallen from Mars or something.'

'You never told me that.'

'Whatever,' I said and put the handle and the canisters over Jasmina's shoulders and started to whistle a tune. She laughed and I scampered down the street, every now and then swimming into the snow that was growing thicker all the time. I cast clumsily-made snowballs, which exploded into thousands of shiny feathers as they hit shuttered shops windows and broken street lights, vanishing like fireflies coruscating in the air.

I stopped at the cistern, in front of a straight line of sour-faced people. 'Look at this shit. It'll never stop. I feel I'd fuck anybody or anything to get out of the whole mess. Lara was so damn lucky with that old Smurf.'

'At least you look good. Who'd want this?' Jasmina grabbed her own flat breasts and then her butt. I put both my hands inside my jacket pretending to have big balloons myself and played a little. 'Oh Monsieur Blue Coat, would you please rip me out of my beloved motherland.'

Jasmina guffawed but the other people in the queue sneered at us. I put a finger over her mouth, giggling. Jasmina choked a laugh.

Half an hour later, I waved goodbye to Jasmina and walked back alone with the full canisters yoked over my shoulders. A mile down the street, I bumped into a middle-aged man, let's call him Sadik. He pulled his bulky stomach in, tightened the wool scarf that was dangling over his chest, straightened his marine blue shirt inside a beige leather jacket, and with all his fingers combed his greasy hair backwards. He looked pretty much like the late sovereign Tito in his Partisan years. He said with the biggest grin, 'You need a hand?'

'No thanks.'

'Come on, you can barely walk. Let me help you with that one.'

Sadik pulled one canister off the broom handle. I lost balance and fell backwards. He was flustered. 'Sorry sorry

sorry.' His hair became unwieldy and his greasy locks glued to his already sweaty forehead. He even managed to pierce one of the canisters against the crumbled kerb and I kicked it. 'Shit. Look what you've done. Mum will kill me.'

'Watch your language.'

I took the broom and stuck it under his nose. I hissed, 'Back off!' Then I started to move away from him, clutching the canister that was still in one piece.

He cried, 'Hey, wait. I'm sorry. It's my fault. Please come back.'

When I was thirty meters away from him, the magical words came. 'Wait, I'll pay for the water.'

I went stiff.

Later, we were sitting in his office. It turned out he ran a travel agency, which was decorated with phony greenish neon letters from the Eighties: 'Fly with Sadik'. He had the same in miniature on the wall behind him. He also had a low, small desk scattered with papers and a multi-colour pen. There was an old computer, one of those first and totally worthless Commodore machines, well, hardly a machine. The white-washed walls were uncomfortably naked and cold, in spite of the colourful photo of the former President put between two bleached posters of a beach with a palm bending all the way down to the foamy water.

'Nice, huh?' he said through his big white teeth. His breath was fresh like mint. I wondered how he managed that.

I said, 'Very.'

'I wouldn't mind going there myself.'

'Why don't you?'

'Have to help people. It's my holy duty as a citizen of this beautiful city that is being destroyed piece by piece.'

He fetched us both a beer. I took a sip and held back a retch. I hated beer, the drink of real men. 'How does running a travel agency in the middle of a war help anyone? Are people taking a week or two of vacation from all this shit?'

'You're clever. I like that.' He fidgeted with his pen, changing the colours and testing each and every one by drawing squiggles. 'People are trapped in the city. There are few channels through which they can escape and move abroad.'

'Tell me something I don't know.'

'Here's the trick. The travel agency is a cover. I get people out of here for good. I send them on a lifelong vacation to Germany, Austria, the US, Scandinavia, Malaysia, Pakistan, Afghanistan, China, you name it.'

I started to sweat like an old bitch and almost let my tongue fall out of my mouth to cool myself and ventilate. Back then, one warm word was enough to set my imagination going. From the hint of a smile behind that mask of professionalism, I could tell that he knew he'd broken my defence.

I gathered myself and said, 'You are fucking with me.'

'No, not at all, well not yet anyway.'

I thought, what the hell. I nudged the water canister with my knee and it glided a little. There was a small pool on the sand-coloured floor. I could already imagine myself running around on that beach, which ought to be fresher than in that picture, drinking and eating that all-exotic stuff, wearing fashionable clothes, walking like people on a catwalk. Mum could do whatever she wanted. Maybe he wouldn't take her with us. Shit.

I rose, picked up the canister, which kept slipping from my sweaty hands, and hurdled myself over the high threshold by saying, 'I have to think about it.'

'So, you don't want to join the happy company.'

'I don't know. It's kind of strange, you know.'

'Don't worry. Let Mr. Sadik here take good care of you. No problem. Let me just make a phone call and I'll get back to you.'

He gave me that smile with a wink again and now I was the one fidgeting around. Before making the call, Sadik pulled a small heater out from a drawer and turned it on. I inched toward the desk. 'You have electricity?'

'Only for my special guests.'

'Wow. That's awesome. Really. How does it work?'

He opened the drawer further and showed me a hidden chaos of wires and small contraptions glued together and attached to a huge lorry battery and a little petrol-driven generator.

'You really know what you're doing, right?'

He grabbed my hands and pulled them closer to the heater. Then he picked up the phone and dialled, all the while glancing and smiling at me. He said to someone on the other line, 'Hi there, you old bastard. How's it going? Fine fine, everything's smooth. Listen, I have a client here. Yeah, exactly, ready for a flight. I mean you know me, a man's got to do what a man's got to do.' Then he interrupted the conversation and turned to me. 'You're over eighteen, right?'

I nodded.

He went on, 'No problem. Maybe you can help us out a little, what do you say? All right, see you later alligator.' He put the phone down. I wriggled in the yellow, steel chair, pulling wry faces the way an actor might before walking out onto the stage. He gave me that wink and smile again and I wondered if I'd come out cheap. I used to do it for drinks and old records of the Stones. It'd been a while since I'd last got laid and I was feeling kind of rusty and tight. Well, tight was always appreciated, but perhaps not too tight and, besides, I'd been having regular haemorrhoid attacks for two months. I was trying not to be shy while looking intensely at the tall Sadik as he went to check if the door was properly bolted. A gust of wind brought some snow into his face and hair and he shook it off and dried the water from his face with his sleeves. His shirt, patched at the elbows, came off. I was starting to have a little crush on him.

The scene started without words. We both knew what exchange of gifts was going to take place. I was impressed by the bulk in his crotch. He pulled me up from the steel chair, pressed my back rather gently until I was bent over the desk, and he whispered, 'Don't mind the papers. Take a grip of anything you need.' Strangely enough, he suddenly smelled of grass, or no, it was more like hay, that was it, hay, as if we were rolling in some country stable.

I dragged down my jeans, revealing my naked butt. Not hesitating for even a split second, he straightened, unbuttoned his trousers, and leaned over me, anchoring into my warm embrace like a skilful sailor, releasing the sound of pleasure of a lost explorer who finally fell upon an oasis. I looked up at the poster of the beach and Tito's portrait and moaned in pain but dragged him hard to me. It felt like short, sharp cuts. Lukewarm fluid ran down my thigh. The lingering pain rippled to the edges of my body, imposing a sense of being cuddled. Then he put his big hand between my legs and massaged me.

We lay content over the desk, he over me, our bodies twitching from time to time until our limbs relaxed and we turned on our sides. I watched him, his eyes still closed and his facial muscles contracting as if in pain. He said, 'This is just what I needed. It's like getting rid of a yoke I've had on me since the war started. You were great. The best I've had in a long time.'

'You were pretty good, too.' I smiled. 'I'm so glad I met you.'

'Yeah,' he said, pulled his pants up, straightened his hair and took a long swig of the beer.

'You could leave this business and go with me.'

He lifted up his head a little, his eyes almost crossed, his expression that of a businessman. 'What the hell are you talking about? We? Very funny. Nobody's going anywhere.'

'What?'

'You didn't really think I could fix you out of here, stupid? Ha, you're amazing. If I could, I'd get the hell out of here myself. Go with me.'

'Of course I did. You said . . . I mean we, we just—'

'I just shagged you, silly. It doesn't mean I want to share my life with you or anything. I'm fucking married.'

'You asshole!' I pushed him and he hit a wall and began to laugh. The poster of the beach fell down. I shouted. I had nothing else to come up with but the plain old 'Fuck you.'

'I just did.'

I darted out into the snow. Somehow, it seemed warmer outside and I started to sweat. Sadik threw out my canister. I stood there for a moment, then jerked up the canister, and started walking across the city, skilfully navigating through safe zones. In an alley close to the Holiday Inn, reporters were fondling some girls. Up in suburbia, I saw two boys quarrelling. Somebody cried 'Fight' and a bunch of boys and girls appeared from nowhere, making a ring around the two fighters. Then, before you could say 'jiffy,' the fight was over and they dispersed.

Walking back up my street, I noticed nothing out of the ordinary. Every face looked the same like when you watch an old Chinese film for the first time and the people all look like clones. I guess we look like clones to them too, if they are following this war on the news.

It was an average afternoon: people passing by, no one laughing; women coming back from imagined bazaars dragging empty bags; children wading in oil pools around burnt cars, some of them dashing off to their homes then coming back running and waving buttered slabs of hard bread; mongrels barking-yelping-squeaking when chased by the kids; cats lying silently on garbage piles like small guardian sphinxes; occasional sniper shots missing or hitting their mark, their accuracy probably depending on the brandy reserves up there in the Jewish cemetery.

The only new thing was some lost peasant yelling at his horse, which was struggling to pull a cart overloaded with firewood that the man was trying to sell to other penniless people. He lashed the animal over the legs and groin. It sounded like glass breaking. The horse was almost burying its head into the ground like an ostrich. The man cried in a shrill voice, 'Jihaah, lad, jihaah! Up with the head!' He then took a tin, went over to the feeble runnels of thawing snow dripping from the roof of a closed-down grocer, filled the tin, drank from it, filled it once more, and poured the stream over the horse's head. It snapped open its big black eyes, shook off the fluid, neighed as if it was going to increase its pace, then dropped down onto its front legs. The children ran around it, shirking the eyes of the owner and yelling, 'Come on, lad! Come on!' The horse jumped up and pulled onwards.

That cheered me up and I ran up four flights of stairs to our flat. Mum was still where I'd left her, at the kitchen table. On a huge plate she'd neatly put two sardines. 'Where's the other canister?'

'A soldier pushed me around and punched a hole in it. He said I was trying to go before others in the queue.'

'Motherfucker,' she said.

I smiled

'Ah, never mind, it's not your fault. Why did it take you so long? It's almost night.'

'I was with Jasmina.'

'Is Jasmina your new girlfriend?'

'No Mum, we're just friends.'

'Pity, she's such a great girl. I mean she's not pretty but she's nice. I know it sounds crazy, but I keep thinking about little feet, you know.'

'Knock it off Mum.' I took both fish into my mouth at the same time.

'Hey, your jeans are wet.'

I felt my behind and it was all wet and sticky. I said quickly, 'I slipped and fell into a pool downtown.'

'Go take them off.'

I went to the small bathroom, looked at myself in the broken mirror, took off my jeans and smelled them. I threw them into a corner, grabbed my buttocks and moaned in pain. I scratched my testicles and checked my butt in the mirror and put on my long johns.

Then Mum came in with a chair. 'Come here. That haircut's

awful. Let me fix it.'

I stared at her as she poured a little water into a bowl and put it on under the tap that hadn't seen water for a year. I laughed when she spruced my face a little and pulled me back to sit down. I took a piece of the broken mirror and tried out a few smiles. Mum dipped her hands into the water and ruffled my hair. I stopped her hand for a second and caressed it.

BUTTER

The crack in the ceiling isn't too bad, but I fear my mother's singing of Bosnian folk songs will tear it open and expose our amazing family to the cold Swedish sky. That'd be great. Then I'd have to move out.

I guess that's what being a refugee means for me, staying with my widowed, menopausal mother ad infinitum. If I didn't live with her, I'd have a girlfriend, maybe, that's what Mum's been telling every single person who enters our home, 'Adam will never move out. He gets fresh and free meals, I wash his clothes, and he's too scared of the big bad world out there.' I guess she's right. Five years ago, I was eighteen and ready to leave home. I was accepted into the flight academy in Belgrade, but then the war broke out and those Yugoslav fighter jets I was supposed to fly now bombed my city. My father became a soldier, hopelessly trying to shoot down planes with a Kalashnikov, until they shot back. A coincidence, of course. I doubt a pilot could ever see an ant with a puny weapon. He was aiming at the entire neighbourhood. I spent those warm war days hunched close to Mum, burning our book collection to keep the fire alive. The annals of late Tito's life were the best fuel.

Mother has changed. She used to be sensible like Grandma Safiya, but now she spends her time on Dr. Phil and her money on make-up, stupid parties, like my barely-legal sister Dunja and her Swedish girlfriend Ulrika. My mother thinks heaping on the make-up will cover the brown bags hanging under her eyes, which she earned during a three-year crying spell after Father died. She looks like the Joker's bride.

My grandma, on the other hand, wears her wrinkles with pride and humility. Yes, she does. Before the war, I spent winter and summer breaks with Grandma in her village. She taught me how to ride a cow, catch snakes in the high grass and use their poison to make concoctions strong enough to kill rats, but not the cats that might eat them. Also, she used to buy me a shitload of comics with the money she made selling cottage cheese.

Grandma lives in prison now. I mean it's a former prison building that a local genius architect turned into a home for the elderly. She hasn't seen much of Sweden. She suffered a stroke in 1993, on her first morning in the southeastern town of Ystad, the port of call for thousands of Bosnians back then. We were being lodged in a hangar. Five hundred beds with disposable paper blankets and pillowcases. It was a military facility, I think, temporarily used to gather the bulk of Balkan refugees before sorting them out according to whatever mysterious categories the government fashioned, and then dispatching them to villages-towns-cities all over the Northern hemisphere. 'Stroke,' the bearded Swedish doctor had said, but a few weeks later Grandma diagnosed herself with bird-strike, or more specifically, a seagull-strike. She told us she woke up at five a.m. on March 8, to celebrate International Women's Day with a sabbah prayer. She went to the bathroom that was larger than her old house, performed a ritual washing, and went out to see if there was a spot of soft grass where she could lay her prayer mat. She looked through the fence at the black horizon over the dark sea, and felt thirsty. As she heaved a deep breath, a dead seagull plummeted down on to her head. There was no need to check these facts.

A month later we moved to the Bible belt, the county around the sea-sized lake Vättern. I insisted that grandma stay with us in the same apartment, that she get a room of her own, a window of her own, and a small desk of her own to hold a lamp and her worn copy of the Qur'an.

Mother voted for a home for the elderly. Easy for her to kick out her mother-in-law. Her vote counted for at least three because she spoke for my late father and grandfather, who'd both ended up in a mass grave around Srebrenica.

I said, 'But she won't like it there. She can't speak Swedish. Why don't you just take her out of her misery.'

'She's like a cat, always has been. Throw her from a plane and she'd land on her feet.'

It's 1998 now. Grandma never comes to us. We (read: me) go to see her occasionally.

I go the bathroom. Mother, my sister Dunja and her girlfriend Ulrika are standing in the steam. They banned me from it, so I shower at work, with the other forklift drivers. Mother is rejuvenating her face for the evening concert with the Balkan crooner, Dino Merlin. He's the biggest Bosnian pop singer and this is his first concert in Sweden. Even skinny Ulrika chants his new song about the plight and nostalgia of refugees, 'Ah, can a bird find its nest, can a refugee find her home.' Bloody shit.

I don't quite get what my sister sees in Ulrika. The two of them are like museum examples of racial difference. Ulrika is tall and breastless, with hair like that of the white queen. Dunja is short and fat, her skin is white, but her hair is so black it eats light. I once imagined them in bed and it grossed me out for a week. I pass by the bathroom on the way to the kitchen. Mother is putting some green goo and cucumbers on her face. I say to her, 'Don't forget to trim your moustache.'

She hurls the jar with the green stuff at me. I catch it and put it gently on the floor, smiling, and she comes and snatches it back.

In the kitchen, I pour myself some sour milk, but it's too thick so I mix it with some water. I put some stew in a plastic canister, wrap a piece of whole-wheat bread, and put everything in a paper bag. I look out at the building site closer by the waterfront. A woman parks a truck near a hole in the ground that looks like a meteor crater. I imagine fumes welling up and a little boy or girl climbing out of the crater with an innocent smile. The woman wipes her hands against her green-yellow overalls and waves to me. I smile and wave back.

I stand with the paper bag outside the open bathroom door. Mother is applying several types of anti-wrinkle goo, different stuff for different parts of the face. I wonder, how different can the skin under the eyes be from the forehead from the chin from the cheeks from the temples?

'Grandma puts butter on her face.' I say. 'She's all yellow and shiny when she's done.'

Mother chortles.

'She still uses butter. I saw her open a big pack and dig up a chunk with her forefinger. She applied it to her face, neck, hands, and up to her elbows.'

'And who's using all the lotions I bought her?'

'I think she throws them away and the nurses pick them up for themselves.'

'That old hag.'

Ulrika looks at me then down at the floor.

I say, 'But grandma keeps telling me to buy her putar. It sounds like 'butter,' but no matter which kind I bring her, she makes that sad face, and says, 'No no, that's not it.' Then, she looks down on the floor for a minute, and says, 'Ah, never mind.''

'Come on, Adam. You must know what putar is. You weren't so young when we fled Bosnia.'

I pretend I suddenly remember, as I always do with things Bosnian, like with the names of people I should know.

Dunja sniggers at me. 'You're no true Bosnian if you don't remember putar. I wouldn't put it on my face but on hot bread, with salt and pepper, wash it down with sour milk. Heavenly.'

Dunja laughs. 'Never mind Adam, he's fallen from the sky. He has no history. He remembers nothing. While I still dream about our old house, the smells, the sounds of the river, he only remembers some incident with stray dogs chasing him. Pathetic.'

Mother says, 'Putar is butter, my dear. But fresh, homemade. You can't buy it here.'

Ulrika says, 'I think they make it on real farms. You should check.'

Dunja says, 'Don't feed his fantasies, sweetie.'

'Thanks, Ulrika. I'll check the *Yellow Pages*.'

Dunja looks at her girlfriend and, seeing Ulrika smiling at me, she shows me her teeth. I grin.

Mother says, 'It's not so hard to make, but you need this wooden canister, whatsitcalled, a butter churn. What you get is this white, soft putar. You use the buttermilk to bake a special kind of bread. Ah, I can smell the fumy bread and feel melting putar on my fingers.' Then she slurped.

'Grandma must feel the same.'

Mother says, 'Never mind your grandma. She's just old and can't adjust. We've integrated, you know. Accepted our putar-less lives.' Then she laughs and continues working with her face.

I grab the *Yellow Pages*, go down to my grey and grumpy but trustworthy Golf '95, and sit with the book open against the steering wheel. There's a listing for a dairy farm not fifteen miles from our house. I dial the number from my first cell phone, saying, 'Nokia, connecting people.'

A deep male voice answers, 'Yes, who is it?'

'Is this Mr. Rolf Smör?

'What do you want?'

'My name is Adam. I need your help with something.

'Is that right?'

'Yeah, I really do, preferably today, if that is all right with you.'

'You're not one of those corporate bastards, are you? You

just want to check up on me, right, see if I feed my cows your shit or let them graze now and then, huh? I saw what you did with Björn and Anna-Lena.'

'I assure you, I'm not a corporate bastard. Please, let me explain. I really mean no trouble.'

'Why do you speak like that? You're not from Jönköping, are you?'

'Unfortunately, no.'

'You sound like a kid. How old are you?'

'I'm—'

'Never mind, lad. I'm just pissed-off about a thing that happened to my neighbour. Shoot.'

'Shoot what?'

'Ask. Tell me what you need.'

'Um, I have an old, sick grandma.'

'So?'

'I need you to produce this special kind of butter. You know, old fashioned, with a churn.' I heard a sound of metal against concrete, as if he dropped a pitchfork.

'That's most unusual. Let me think. I may have one churn left. Got it from my father when I took over the farm. Brings up a lot of memories, you know.'

I stuttered, 'Do you think you can find it?'

Silence.

'Mr. Smör?'

'Yeah, sure. What did you say you needed it for, your granny?'

'Yes.'

'Hm, you really took me by surprise, kid. Tell you what, I'll dig up the old thing soon as I've seen to my pretty ladies, so come by whenever you can. I'll be around.'

'Thank you so much. I really appreciate it. You're very kind.'

'Ah, no trouble at all.'

'Thanks.'

At the home for the elderly, I punch the code at the door and there's a click. As I step in, freckled Malin, the nurse responsible for Grandma, walks by with a tray and brushes me with her elbow. 'Hi, Adam. Good to see you.'

'Hey, hey.' I glance at her cleavage. 'Good to see you, too.'

She goes into the kitchen, sits at a table and starts spoon-feeding a bald man with an empty look in his eyes. 'There you go. Now roll your tongue and swallow your porridge.' She tickles his throat until he gulps.

I stand there, watching the ritual-like process, until she looks up at me with her big blue eyes and says, 'Your grandma's in her room.'

'Of course. Thanks.'

I step into Grandma's room as if into an office. She is by the window, seated in her wheelchair, talking loudly on the phone in Bosnian, 'Why do you keep answering the phone? Put my grandson on! Who are you? What? I don't understand a word you're saying. Police? What police? I'll send you the police, you hag.' She slams down the receiver.

I touch her on the shoulder. 'Grandma, who were you talking to?'

'Adam, thank God you're here. Some weird woman is answering your phone. I've been calling you for days since you changed your number. She won't let me speak with you.'

'Grandma, there's no weird woman where I live.' I laugh, thinking, Actually, there are two, but they wouldn't speak Swedish with you. They won't even answer the phone when they see your number on the display. I ask her, 'What number did you call?'

She pulls a scrunched piece of blue napkin from her bra.

'Aha,' I said, 'some numbers are smudged. It should be 50, not 60. Did you blow your nose with this napkin?'

She throws the paper on the ground. 'Go ahead, make fun of your grandma.'

I hug her. 'Don't be mad. Just kidding a little.'

I comb her unwieldy hair with my fingers and shape it into

a ponytail. 'Listen Grandma, you need to come with me. I've got a surprise for you. We must leave now.'

'I can't. I need to perk up and wait for my escort.'

'What are you talking about?'

'This new fellow in 305, Haris. He's from Sarajevo. He's taking me to see Dino Merlin tonight. He's Dino's relative so we'll get good seats on the balcony and even go backstage to talk with the young man.'

'Et tu, Brute.'

'What did you say?'

'That's so cool, I mean, good for you, but listen, there's time to get pretty. Let's first go someplace else. I promise it's worth it. You're worth it.'

'Just don't embarrass me.'

'Fat chance.'

My Golf glides over the blooming countryside. Grandma is in the passenger seat, complaining about stomach ache. 'Dear boy, I've been having these nasty diarrhoeas for a week now.'

'Grandma please, there's no toilet for another five miles.'

'I'm sweating, and when I start sweating, there's not much time left.'

I pull off the road and park between a few trees. Before I help her out, I take the paper towels I use to clean the windshield. 'Hold this.' Between slender birch trees, I remove the huge nappy, and hold her under her armpits until she is finished. She wipes herself. I move her a few steps away from the crime scene, place the nappy between her legs and pull up her panties and the skirt.

'Bless you.'

'No trouble, Grandma. Any time.'

Back in the car, Grandma combs her hair, licks her thumb and strokes her eyebrows. She says, 'Why won't you tell me what this is all about?'

'It's a surprise.'

'I hate surprises.'

'You'll like this one.'

'I'm sure I won't.' For a second I lose control and the car swerves into the opposite lane, but I get it straight again.

She says, 'I must dress nice for tonight.'

'Grandma, let's just do this. One shot, that's all I'm asking.'

She grabs my chin and shakes it. 'Whatever makes you happy.'

I smile. 'Over there, that must be it.'

I stop in front of a small yellow cottage. A woman with black glasses throws corn to salt-'n-pepper hens and newly-hatched chicks, which keep stumbling over small rocks and falling on their beaks. The smell of grass and shit and linden sweeps over the gravel. I touch Grandma's brow and say, 'I'll be right back, I say and I get out of the car and stride over to the woman.

'Mind the hens,' she says.

'Of course, I'm sorry. Is Mr. Smör at home?'

'He's cleaning the dung. Over there.' She points at a long Dala-red stable with a door left ajar.

'Thank you.'

I jump over the hens that gather around my feet, run the few yards, and peer in. A farmer is shoving cow dung into a wheelbarrow.

'Mr. Smör?'

The seven-foot man stretches up and wipes his forehead with a dirty sleeve.

'I'm Adam. We spoke on the phone.'

'Yes, the butter boy. Come on in. Admire my ladies a little. Give them compliments and they'll give you the best milk, for the best cheese and cream and butter and what not. You know, I once read milk and oil are the only two things whose waste product is useful.'

'That's very . . . '

'Milk is pure. It's good. Oil is evil. If God intended us to use oil, he wouldn't have buried it deep underground.'

I keep a straight face. 'Couldn't agree more.'

He sniffs at the air, looks around as if something unexpected just sneaked in, and he says, You're the boy?'

'I'm the boy.' I point at the car through the open door. 'That's my grandma over there in the car.'

He looks out, waves at Grandma and grins, and then he points at a two-foot tall wooden churn, made of reddish cherry wood, and girded with three black, metal rings.

'Wow, that's brilliant. Grandma will love it.'

He rubs his face with both palms and says, 'I'll go and fetch the cream.'

I help Grandma out and lead her to a bench in front of the stable. She says, 'It smells like home here. Look at those crazy hens chasing that calf over there.' Grandma laughs, but there's no sound.

I laugh and stroke her hunched back. I show her the churn. 'All right Grandma, this is what we're here for. We'll make real butter so you can eat it, apply it to your wrinkles, whatever you want.'

'That's not my churn. Mine is slender and tall, like my late Rasim. Three-feet at least. He made it for my thirtieth birthday. It smelled nice.'

'This churn is good, too. Let's try it.'

'Do as you want.'

Mr. Smör comes back with the cream, pours it into the churn, makes sure the lid is properly sealing the opening, and places it between Grandma's legs. She says, 'No.'

The farmer looks at her like at an old photograph.

I say, 'I'll do it for you.' I kneel in front of her and work it hard. Grandma stares at me. I open the lid after about twenty minutes. Mr. Smör brings us another canister to pour out the buttermilk. Grandma puts her fingers under the stream and then licks them. She shrugs.

I take a big nugget of butter, like white gold, and give it too her.

She puts it into her mouth and chews it a little. Then she rubs it into her face, behind her ears, and on her breasts. She puts some more on the bags under her eyes.

Mr. Smör hunches next to us, waiting.

Grandma looks at him, all shiny. She says in Swedish, 'Tackar så hjärtligt.'

Mr. Smör smiles at her. 'Varsågod.'

She smiles back at him, nods and says, 'Jätte snällt.' Then she turns to me. 'I need to get dressed.'

'Absolutely.'

Around 10 p.m. Grandma is looking all bloomy in her new dress. I drive her wheelchair into the small concert hall crammed with dancing teenagers. Malin drives Haris's wheelchair. The old people are holding hands. We find the booked places on the balcony. A small round table for two. Merlin is jumping on the stage singing about Bosnian blossom. Grandma points at her dress and sings with him, 'Bosnom behar probeharao.'

Malin laughs, and says, 'Adam, I have to leave now. Will you be all right?'

'I think I can deal with two old farts.'

Malin leans over Grandma and says, 'All right, Safiya, I'm going now. Have a nice evening.'

'Tack. Ses imon.'

'Hej då.'

I spot my mother dancing with someone, a man, slightly shorter than she, their big bellies pressed against each other. Dunja is sulking in a corner close to the entrance and Ulrika hugs her from behind and kisses her ear. Then a chubby little waitress puts two Fanta bottles with straws in front of the old couple.

I say, 'Thanks. Can you please get me one too?'

'You're not drinking?'

'No, I'm driving.' I point at the wheelchairs.

'OK.'

Grandma sings a little more and drinks half her Fanta, and then she starts sweating, and she looks up at me with her mouth open.

I say, 'Let's go.'

She avoids her date's eyes as I drive her to the toilet. She does her thing, and I bring her back to their table, where she smiles at Haris, but then I see he's breaking into a sweat as well. I say, 'Grandma, can I borrow your guy for a sec?'

'Just bring him back in one piece.'

Haris doesn't smile at her joke, and as I drive him to the toilet, He reaches out behind him until he puts his big hand on mine. 'Thank you.'

'You'd better be good to her. No funny business.'

We both laugh and I notice the chubby waitress, who overheard us, is laughing as well.

Haris takes his time in the loo and I stand outside, leaning against a blue concrete wall. The waitress comes to me. 'Hey there. How're you doing?'

'Good.'

She nods a few times. 'So, you're a carer?'

'Not really. That's my grandma, and her, date.'

'Good for her. She's got one bloke more than I.'

I say nothing.

'My grandma is dead.'

'Sorry to hear that.'

She hands me a glass of beer.

'I didn't order any.'

She laughs and takes it back and looks around to check where she was supposed to take it, but she doesn't leave. She says, 'Anyway, how do you like Merlin's new stuff?'

'Tacky.'

'Really? I love it. It's heartbreaking.'

I scratch some part of my face that does not itch, but feels like it's going to any second. 'It's OK, I guess. It's just too damn nostalgic. Cheap.'

'You know how to butter up a girl, don't you?'

'I, didn't, think, I mean . . . what do you mean?'

Haris knocks on something inside and calls my name, but

I don't go in.

'Your friend is calling.'

'Yes. He is. But, I mean, you're right. Dino's OK, I guess.'

'Adam. I'm done. Come on now.'

Speaking through the keyhole, I say, 'Just a sec, Haris.' When I look up at the waitress, she's already on her way back to the bar where a man with a huge crooked nose is signalling her to fetch the drinks, and I go inside to help Haris.

Back at the table, Grandma has finished her Fanta and is wriggling her lips as if she just put on some lipstick. Haris starts working on his soda right away, then cocks up his ear when a new song begins. 'Safiya, this one is for you. I asked Merlin to do it.'

She caresses his hand on the cold glass, and they sing along until about halfway through the song, then Grandma starts signalling she needs to go again.

Again, I lean on the wall and laugh at the way Grandma's grunts inside the toilet mix with the smooth, sentimental song. I look for the waitress. She is at the bar and glances at me. I shrug and smile. She walks towards me even though the bartender is telling her something.

'I have a feeling you'll be going home soon.'

'Yeah, I don't know how much they can take.'

She says, 'I'm Sabina.'

'Adam.'

'Listen, Adam, since you're the only guy here who doesn't drink, I'd need a favour. Is there a chance you can come back and pick me up when the show is over? I mean, once you've taken the old people home. It's just, my boss is drunk already and I hate going with him anyway.'

I stare at her.

'Please.'

'Yes. Of course. I'm a brilliant driver. I have a kick-ass car. Diesel engine.'

She laughs. 'Sounds great. Thanks.'

Merlin begins the refugee ballad. Sabina walks back to her

red-faced boss. Grandma shouts over the music, 'Adam, I'm done.'

I laugh and sing with Merlin as I go into the toilet.

VACATION: A TRAVELOGUE

'there it is, either you love or you don't'
— Samuel Beckett, 'First Love'

Mother told me I should never love my job. Like my job, now that was socially acceptable behaviour. Love it — that was too much.

I did all kinds of work when I came to Sweden during the Balkan war. I was seventeen. I took Swedish lessons in the morning. In the afternoon I mended fences, hosed down dirt from pink pigs, did the night-watch at the textile factory, sold old records and hand-me-down guitars, painted school corridors. I did not love those jobs.

Then I got a job that involved a lot of shit and piss and disease. Loved it.

I became a carer to an old man in a wheelchair. Stefan. But I like to call him my Swede. He'd had a stroke.

Stefan was a calm man who slept a lot, cherished his silences, and honed the art of patience. He listened to audio books for hours and lived for semla day like a true patriot. He was blind in his right eye. His left eye could spot a stray cookie on a bookshelf like a bird spotting its prey. I'd place After Eights all over his apartment and then I'd say, 'Let's take a sightseeing tour, shall we?' I'd drive him from the kitchen, along the oak bookshelves in the corridor, past the toilet, into the room where we care assistants had our own microwave oven and teabags, then on through the flower-less living room and into his bedroom. I'd slow down and say things like, 'And on the right side you can see the angry spirit of Strindberg slowly evaporating . . . ' This meant I'd put polka gris candy on *The Red Room*, which was his favourite. If he missed the hiding place, he'd make a circle in the air with his index finger. 'Another tour, please.'

In the evenings, we watched TV for hours. We loved old thrillers but he, despite his high education, had a peculiar penchant for crappy Swedish crime dramas. Since I was studying literature and philosophy on the side, I once played a smartass and said, 'Maybe the simple plotting offers some existential structure to your broken life?'

'You're becoming too academic, boy. God help you. You should write some simple erotic poetry as an antidote.'

He showed me some poems about oral sex and damaged condoms. I laughed my ass off.

'I'll leave you these in my will,' he said,

'Oh, really? Thanks. That's cool.'

'I need to piss.' Most of the time, he did not really need to. He was just bored.

DIES SOLIS

My Swede bought a 7-day trip to Cyprus for 11 September 2007. This vacation, our sixth, the care team consisted of two women and myself. His vacation would be mine too. I'd have a whole 24 hrs off between my shifts. 'Luxury,' I said to the others who were worried it would be too hard. 'I used to be the only one on earlier trips, I worked 24/7.' One of the carers, Frida, the nice one, the pretty one, the chubby one, packed his bags and came with him to the airport. My wife packed my bag: old clothes, socks, underwear, T-shirts, shorts. She said, 'Don't bring these rags back.' I filled the rest of the bag with books, *My Mistress' Sparrow is Dead*, a collec-tion of greatest love stories selected by Jeffrey Eugenides,

Ethics of Identity by K.A. Appiah, my iPod, and my iBook.

I went to bed past midnight and catnapped for an hour and a half. I had a dream in which my Swede was out of his wheelchair, running on a beach chased by his other carer, big-breasted Helga. What a way to recover, huh?

MOON DAY

At 2:10 a.m., Helga came in her red Nissan Micra to drive us to Arlanda airport.

I did not turn down her hugs, and I did not look up at my kitchen window to see if my wife was watching. Helga took her bags out of the trunk and stood trying to figure out how to arrange the luggage. I said, 'Are you moving in with us?'

'Ha, ha.'

I ended up having my briefcase and a bag of hard green apples on my lap.

I've suppressed the memory of what we talked about on the way to Arlanda. On the motorway, her Micra behaved like a schoolgirl, unfocused and disobedient. Something cracked under my seat and I muttered a prayer.

At the airport, I didn't turn down Frida's hugs either. She hugs people all the time. It's like a tic, it doesn't mean anything. My Swede gave me a big smile. I loved that smile. Especially after he lost one of his incisors. He looked so funny when he grinned, his grey beard covering his thin lips, like a character from the Italian comics I read as a kid.

There were eight people in wheelchairs altogether, all hiring help from a private company called JAG. Boarding them all delayed the flight one hour. One of them had a body so contorted he had to lie down on the laps of his three girls.

Stefan wanted to go to the toilet a couple of times during the flight, which was impossible, so I reminded him, 'Pee in your nappy.'

He half slept, listening to Hemingway's *For Whom the Bell Tolls* on my iPod. We both loved Hemingway. The old man's prose was something of an icebreaker when I first met him. I carried around a collection of Hemingway's short stories to impress girls, which only gave me hardboiled rejection-rhetoric. I had it with me on my job interview, and Stefan had nodded and smiled, like a father proud of his kid.

That was one of the reasons I stayed with him through the worst crises, months when he was mad at everyone and kept changing his carers like nappies. I didn't leave him, even when I was scared shitless I would get his Hepatitis C while cleaning him up, dressing the pressure sores on his arse.

It was hot in Cyprus when we arrived. My Swede went straight to a small toilet in his room at the hotel. He was so happy to finally be able to piss.

I told Helga, 'This toilet is ridiculous.'

'Awful. I'll go talk to the management.'

Nothing happened. We didn't change rooms. No apology. Helga said, 'We should steal their towels and little bottles of conditioner.'

'Yes, that should teach them a lesson.'

At 7 p.m., I served him food at the cosy, saffron-coloured restaurant where waiters of all nationalities served an international buffet.

TIWESDÆG

It was my day off, so I went out after breakfast. The town was awful. It was like walking along a DNA spiral with certain recurring patterns: restaurant-realtor-souvenirs-restaurant, in different colours (blue-white, ochre-white). There was a Chinese palace, an Egyptian bar, Irish pubs that had drag shows, Italian pizzerias, Thai food, a Flintstones place and a huge wigwam called Red Indian. Authentic stuff.

Like a good old explorer, I climbed a hill to gain some vantage points, but halfway up a black lizard crossed the goat path right in front of me, and I turned back.

I walked walked walked, then after seeing big-bellied, bare-chested Germans, I took off my T-shirt, and walked walked walked some more. Finally, I clambered up the steps up a cliff to an old orthodox chapel. I gave up counting the steps halfway up. Three trees around the chapel had hundreds of ribbons with names and a few photos of old people and even kids. I didn't read the inscriptions of lovers' names carved on the oak door. Inside, the wall paintings were no old frescoes, but rather dull modern oil paintings of JC and some other characters. I uttered a prayer and went out.

Half an hour later, my wife called me and said she was pregnant, again. We had four boys and were really working hard on a girl. We'd had a girl name ready for years. I said, 'I have a feeling it'll be a boy this time, too.' She hung up.

Before dinner, I dressed my patient in a nice green shirt and large black pants. We sat outside the restaurant waiting for the others to join us. I sent my wife a few text messages: I'm sorry, Love you, Sorry again.

My Swede stared at a squirrel playing with a green hose.

I said, 'I'm sorry I was playing with the phone. I had a call earlier, and, well, I'm gonna be a father for the fifth time. So the dinner's on me.'

He laughed, nodded, looked at the squirrel again and then back at me. 'That's great, my boy. I envy you. I grew up in a big family. Now I have an ex-wife.'

'You got me old man.' I patted him on the knee. 'We'll celebrate after dinner with a huge strawberry milkshake,' which was his all-time favourite.

'Deal.'

The Chinese dinner was awful. My Swede wielded his toothpick like a sword to remove the piece of beef stuck between his teeth. He said, 'I need to piss.' In the men's room, I saw he'd already wet his pants. He looked at the floor as if this had never happened before. I said, 'Don't worry. I almost did it myself.'

DAY OF HERMES

At 8 a.m. Helga came over. Her hair was all messy and her breasts were not quite kept in check by that little blue bra. She went in to Stefan, leaned over him, her breasts resting on his chest. She pinched his cheeks. 'Hey, sweetie, waky waky, rise and shine.'

I could never sleep after a nightshift, so I went back to the chapel because it was the only place that had any resemblance to some culture. The little bell tolled. Someone shouted and the black bell with Cyrillic inscriptions tumbled a yard from me and all the way down to the beach. I ran after it as if to catch it. It looked as if the sea had washed it out. I thought maybe it had reacted to my Muslim presence or something, but then I remembered I was not superstitious.

I ran back to the hotel, determined not to tell anyone about the incident. Frida and Helga would probably just utter their typical ejaculations, 'Oh no, really?' It didn't matter whether they'd just tasted an unusual sauce with their meatballs or seen the collapse of the Twin Towers.

I sat close to where my Swede and Frida were sunbathing. He kept turning his head, wriggling in his hammock. Frida was snoring.

I put my iPod on his belly and the earplugs in his ears and pressed play.

He nodded.

Then my wife called with the good news, 'I've forgiven you for saying it'll be another boy. I don't really care what it is, as long as she has the right number of fingers and all.'

'Good for me. I was just teasing you, you know that. Love you.'

'Love you, too. And, don't spend too much time with those Swedish women, all right.'

'Of course.'

THOR'S DAY

My Swede sat on the toilet while I rubbed Head and Shoulders into his thin hair. I shaved his face around the goatee and then washed the inflamed spot between his legs. Frida had forgotten to pack the indigo-coloured sterilizer nurse Ulrika had given us. The hot, moist air was making the infection worse. I applied some beeswax ointment, from the survivor's kit I got from my grandma, and put gauze on to prevent skin-to-skin contact.

Breakfast. I ate three croissants with chocolate cream and walnuts, and then some green tea to cleanse my conscience. He munched his favourite blue cheese on toast.

The weather was not promising. There was a strange haze over the sky and we could hear random thunder. I said, 'Maybe we should offer one of these croissants to the Mighty Thor so he cools down for today.'

He didn't react. Then he stuttered, 'I'd like some ice-cream.'

I smiled. 'You know they only serve it after dinner. How about we go get ourselves a strawberry milkshake and spoil our lunch?'

He opened wide his eyes, which were a shade brighter than the cheese.

We spent the afternoon on the beach. I used two sheets from his room to make a tent around him. I put a plastic container under his penis. A German couple gawked at us.

He said, 'Read me something nice.'

'OK.' I opened the Eugenides' anthology. 'Lady with the Little Dog.'

A page later, he was snoring. It worried me that he was sleeping so much lately, more than thirteen hours a day. He barely spoke and he couldn't focus on anything more complicated than a milkshake.

Frida popped by and we talked about having him thoroughly checked. I said, 'Could it be that he gets these bladder infections all the time because he can't pull back his foreskin. It's so tight, as if it's crumpled or something. It's a regular Petri dish in there.'

'Maybe he hasn't had an erection for too long.'

'I don't know. Last time he got this infection, there was greenish stuff running out and the nurse said I should clean it because you girls wouldn't.'

'Ugh.'

'I used those Q-tips to clean inside the foreskin. I couldn't pull it back. I had no idea it was like that.'

Stefan woke up and said, 'Maybe I should get circumcised.'

Frida laughed. 'Maybe you should pick up a hot German tourist.'

FREYA'S DAY

My day off. I couldn't read because my eyes hurt when I lay on the beach. I went inside to watch *The Wire*, which a friend had downloaded for me from The Pirate Bay, but just as I was getting comfortable, Frida came by and said, 'I need your help. He fell when I was moving him to the bed.'

I ran to his room. Stefan was splayed between his bed and the wall. He looked scared, but when he saw me he started laughing.

I put his soles against each other so he'd glide into the right position when I pulled him up onto the bed. 'You're not going to sleep now, are you?'

Frida said, 'He's tired.'

'You're too tired these days, my friend. Let's go down to the beach together and have a swim. The JAG staff brought a special wheelchair that floats in water.'

He nodded.

He thought the water was cold and wanted to get out the same moment we pushed him in, but I made him stay floating for fifteen minutes. This would stimulate his brain and stymie memory loss. I bought him a huge milkshake as a consolation prize.

After dinner, he refused to watch some horrible singers promoting their Abba cult. He went to bed early. He woke up three times (at 02:15; 04:37; 06:12), but I didn't take him to the toilet. Instead he used the canister. His infection smelled so bad he couldn't fall asleep.

'Please open the window.'

'Sure, but first let me kill the lights. You don't want mosquitoes in here.'

I lay on the floor next to him until the stench thinned out and he started snoring.

DAY OF CRONUS

Helga was late that morning. 'Sorry, I overslept.'

'No trouble. I'll give you the report later.' I rushed to make four croissants with chocolate and walnuts, and then went to the beach with my anthology. My wife called to tell me she was vomiting all the time, and that I was an awful man for going on a vacation and leaving her at home pregnant. I said, 'But, I'm working. And besides, you didn't tell me you were pregnant until I got here.' I'm not sure what else she said because after the first volley I stopped listening.

I read Kundera's 'The Hitchhiking Game' and fought small annoying flies at the same time. The story of two lovers playing games with their feelings made me think I should include it in the graduate course 'Love and its Discontents' that I was occasionally teaching in the Department of English. I could teach Kundera along with ee cummings' 'she being brand new.' Six months earlier, an otherwise silent student reproached me for being a male chauvinist for teaching cummings, and I told her that it was, in fact, a female colleague who brought my attention to this poem and taught me how to teach it. This time I had to be more careful, but it bothered me. Words hurt, for God's sake. Literature provokes. 'Fuck it,' I said out loud, 'I'm gonna shape the course any way I fucking want.'

In this post-Kundera mood, I called home and spoke with my oldest son who said he missed me a lot and that he was counting days. I smiled my ridiculous smile, as always when I felt loved. I said, 'Let me talk to your mother.'

She answered, 'What do you want?'

'I love you, so stop busting my ass. I know you're having a hard time vomiting, and if I were there I'd kiss your vomiting mouth to prove it.'

'That's gross, you're nuts.'

'Fucking yeah.'

She laughed and that was it. I felt better. I had a sandwich. Not even the stray cat playing with a half-dead lizard ruined my appetite.

It was windy and I went back to the room. I passed the pool where Frida was having an aerobics session. I filled the small bathtub with hot water. I felt horny and I sat on the edge of the bathtub, my feet scorching in the water. I masturbated thinking of my wife, but it did not work so well because I remembered Slavoj Žižek's essay on masturbation, which he called the only true solipsistic activity. I gave up self-pleasure and enjoyed my bath.

Then I did all my daily prayers at once. Travellers could do that. There were some guidelines as to how all that worked, but I could not remember the rules. I lay out a towel in the approximate direction of Mecca, prayed for twenty minutes, and by the end felt that tinge work its way through my body, and I felt grateful for everything, especially for my Swede, and my wife's pregnancy, of course. Stefan's patience made me want to be a better man, argue less with my wife and scream less at the boys when they eddied through the house like whirlwinds.

Our last evening, I dressed Stefan in a blue, silk shirt and black pants, and joined Frida and Helga at the local Irish pub to watch a drag show. He and I drank non-alcoholic drinks, which were terribly sweet and cold. The drag queen was a dreadful Eddie Izzard rip-off. An hour into the show, he transformed into Dolly Parton and jumped about with enormous tits. Stefan smiled for a second, but then he went on slurping his drink.

ANOTHER DAY OF SUN

Rain. It always rained on the day I went home from a vacation, ever since I was a kid and my parents took me to Croatia. We checked out and spent five hours in the lobby waiting for the bus to take us to the Larnaca airport. I took care of my Swede while my colleagues handled the luggage. The bus driver slapped Frida on her behind. He couldn't speak English, so I pointed at the extra wheelchair in the lobby and he followed me to fetch it. Then I pushed him against a wall and said, 'Listen motherfucker, slap her or any other woman again and I'll cut off your hands.' I don't know what language I spoke, but his eyes betrayed a deep understanding. He silently helped me with the things.

Helga gave our patient his sleeping pills too early. We barely managed to push his über-relaxed body all the way into the window seat. He looked as if his head needed to release gases. I couldn't do anything and he didn't seem to be in pain so I tried to ignore it and let him sleep.

We came home close to midnight. I sent a text message to my wife, 'I'm back.' Stefan went straight to his huge toilet and looked as if that was the single thing he most missed.

Once his head touched the pillow he was already snoring. I looked at him and said, 'Thanks for the trip, my friend.' Then I tucked him in and went to unpack.

THREE WEEKS LATER

After almost eleven years since our first meeting at St. Göran's hospital in Stockholm, the interview to which I was late and did not think I'd get the job, after eleven years of doing what never felt like a job, but more like companionship, eating and laughing together, watching cheesy movies and reading Classics, and respecting each other's silences, my wheel-chaired Swede died. Although he had chest pains over the weekend, he refused to go to the hospital, but then he ended up at the ER on Monday. On Thursday, the nurses told me he could probably hear me, despite the morphine. I read him Beckett's story 'First Love', which is about death, and begins with a man who writes his own epitaph: 'Hereunder lies the above who up below so hourly died that he lived on till now.' I laughed. Beckett was so damn funny. My Swede didn't laugh. He breathed as if he wanted to inhale an extra dose of air to lift him off the bed. His eyes moved as if he was scanning the room. His mouth was white from dried spit. I found some moisturizing mouth-gel, put it on my index finger and applied it to every part of his mouth cavity and his tongue. He didn't react at all. The breathing had a slower, more regular rhythm, until it disappeared.

Then I recited him the Al-Fatiha prayer.

THE LOVERS' DISCOURSE

'No one repairs umbrellas any longer,' Adam said, picked a cherry from a newspaper-cone, ate it, and spat the salty pit into the dirty seawater of Hammarby, the southeast of Stockholm, neither the city nor the suburbs. His wife, Hava, spat hers out, making a series of small rings a foot beyond his.

'Humph,' he said.

She laughed and wiggled her tongue at him and he quickly ate another cherry, rocked his body a couple of times where he sat, then spat out the pit. It won him another foot. 'How 'bout that?'

She caught his mouth with a hook-shaped finger and reeled his head down on her knees. He stretched his body out on the dock boards, his nose facing her navel, and he breathed in her smell: green peppers and vanilla buns. Usually she never smelled of food, even right after a meal, while he could reek of garlic for hours. Bad smells seemed to stick to him like old undesired girlfriends, but if he gulped a basket of strawberries, he would ooze no sweetness. He twisted his head in her lap and looked out over the water toward Skanstull Church. The sun was strong, the harbour wind cold. Sky-scraping cranes moved as if working on an invisible origami of air and sunshine. Closer to the ground, they pulled buildings from the resistant earth. These Stockholm houses were so tight to each other that the neighbours could feel each other's morning breaths.

Adam and Hava had been homeless Bosnians. Five years ago, after he wrote a book about the homelessness of refugees, the Swedes kept asking him, 'Do you ever feel at home?' He would put on his poetic mask and say something like, 'Stockholm kidnapped us in the 90s, when we arrived on refugee buses. Like all good hostages, we eventually fell in love with our captor. This is what Stockholm syndrome means to us.' For him, homelessness was a fashionable, albeit ambiguous, affair. Hava's homelessness was different, unhomely.

Adam lifted up his head from Hava's lap, looked at the washed-out blue of the sky and said, 'No really, I mean, remember when we were kids and Gypsies came to town hollering about umbrellas and whetting knives? They dragged their small carts, a bizarre mix of wheelbarrows, stoves, and God knows what else. People used to repair worn things, renew them. We must have bought a dozen umbrellas since we immigrated to Sweden.' He tilted his head up a little to try to see her, but it felt heavy with the summer flu and it dropped back on her soft thighs. 'Just think about it. It rains or snows almost all the time, and we hardly ever use umbrellas. My mother inherited a red one with a big, white socialist star on it.'

She said, 'I fixed your umbrella.'

'Really? I have one?'

'The black one you bought in New York, with drawings of cats and dogs.'

'I thought I'd lost it.'

'You punched a huge hole in it three months ago.'

'Why would I do that?'

'You got mad with me for being jealous.'

'That's right.'

'I closed the hole with a pink patch. It needed a face lift. Maybe that's why you tore it in the first place. Black is too depressing, even with funny white figures on it.'

He pushed himself up and smiled at her. 'Pink. I like that.'

He kissed her.

A bunch of youngsters were grilling honey-glazed chicken wings and aubergine. Adam stroked his wife's belly. The sweet BBQ smell mixed with the salty sea air and sour exhaust from the nearby motorway.

There is gentleness, Hava thought, in this suffering, this insipid tumult. I fall, flow, melt. I'm dissolved, engulfed, but not dismembered.

She touched his Adam's apple, slowly, the way toes test cold water. He sat up and held his throat as if she'd cut his jugular.

There's work to do, she thought and pulled open a plastic bag full of beefy, bloody cherries, poured them on the ridge, and made two equal heaps. She took the top cherry into her mouth. Red juice ran down her chin. She spat so forcefully her ponytail loosened and her hair tangled around her face. She laughed, pointing at the distant ripples. 'Beat that.'

WHAT WE TALK ABOUT WHEN WE TALK ABOUT SUICIDE

i.
Sep 11, 2010. Chat-room 5. Users present: Mikaella, Jenny, Claes, Björn&Benny, Nicky-Picky.

JENNY: if I eat 15 paracetamol and 20 strattera with half a bottle of vodka, will it work?

CLAES: don't be silly, of course it won't work, you'll just get stomachache

BJÖRN&BENNY: at the most

JENNY: hmmm, i'll try it anyway, once i get back home

NICKY-PICKY: i'll keep my fingers crossed that it works

JENNY: thanks you guys. but, what else could i do, i'm running low on imagination over here ????

CLAES: hang yourself

JENNY: i don't know how

BJÖRN&BENNY: you're pathetic

JENNY: i mean there's nothing in the apartment I could use, maybe i could try one of those trees behind my building

MIKAELLA: but there's a daycare there, u shouldn't scare the kids first thing in the morning. not cool

JENNY: right, that was stupid, thanks M, you're a good

friend

BJÖRN&BENNY: why don't ya take a shotgun to your stupid little mouth

CLAES: or if u go with the pills, then slice ur wrists and fill a bathtub with water and lie there until u bleed to death, or u might drown, who knows

NICKY-PICKY: anyways, we'll all keep our fingers crossed

CLAES: yep, whatever

BJÖRN&BENNY: I'm with ya

MIKAELLA: we're all with you, u go girl

JENNY: alright, bye then

ii

Sep 12, 2010. Chat-room 9. Users present: Cleas, Linda, Zayneb

CLAES: seems Jenny's gonna do herself in

LINDA: u don't mean

CLAES: yeah, but she's so chickenshit, i don't think she'll go through with it

LINDA: u think u can do better

CLAES: i don't much care for that sorta thing, but hell yeah, i could do way better

ZAYNEB: what's the matter with u guys, stop talking about that shit, that's just not cool

CLAES: who the fuck r u?????

ZAYNEB: i have dance lessons with Jenny, she's a nice girl, she's been down is all, she musnt kill herself

CLAES: leave the girl be will ya, mind ur own bizniss

ZAYNEB: it's against my faith, suicide is

CLAES: u the girl with the tent over ur face

LINDA: claes please whatt the

CLAES: u should speak bout suicide fucking Taliban, maybe u cn show her how 2 bomb her sorry ass

LINDA: claes stop it for fuck sake, that's not cool, leave her be

ZAYNEB: U R a BIG ARSE, u know i was born and raised in stockhlm, go fuck youself

CLAES: u got some big fucking mout right there but i'm sure u shut the fuck up in your male dominted home

ADMINISTRATOR: I'm cutting you off. You may not use curse words in this forum.

iii

Sep 15, 2010. Chat-room 1. Users present: Zayneb, Marky-Mark, Shrek, Fiona

ZAYNEB: u guys, have u seen jenny

Shrek: no, she's been away for 2 days at least, why do u ask

ZAYNEB: it's just, that arsehole claes was talking about her killing herself an I thought he was just fucking with us, but she's missed school

FIONA: don't worry, she probly just fine, or maybe has a cold or sth

ZAYNEB: i should've told someone, maybe the nurse what-shername

MARKY-MARK: Linda, yeah she's nice, helped me one time i was in trouble, can't say what it was

ZAYNEB: I should go and see her about it, maybe she can get in touch with the family

MARKY-MARK: that's a good idea, ur a nice girl Z

ZAYNEB: Fiona, do u mind going with me 2 c Linda

FIONA: sure, let's do it after the math tutorial

ZAYNEB: great, thanx

iv

Sep 15, 2010. Chat-room 2. Users present: Cleas, Björn&Benny, Kick-Ass, Chanel Nr 5

BJÖRN&BENNY: so she really did it . . . i thought she ws kidding

KICK-ASS: what R U talking bout

Björn&Benny: Jenny killed herself

Kick-Ass: amazing, i thought she was sick or sthing

Björn&Benny: no, i live next door to her, there's been lotsa crying over there

Claes: really, didn't know eithr, man she's pretty cool after all, how did she do it

Björn&Benny: don't know, but I heard she filmed it with web camera, live feed on youtube but no one saw it at the titme and then they removed it from the net

Claes: it'll probly turn up on the pirate bay or some place, those things cant just be buried, I mean she wasnt fucking CIA or something

Björn&Benny: i know i was fucking with her on that chat, but i don't wanna see it man, why are u into this shit

Claes: just fucking curious

Administrator: Please stop using the F word or I will shut you out.

Kick-Ass: it'd be good to know what she did

Björn&Benny: r u thinking of doing it

Kick-Ass: crossed my mind, a few times

Björn&Benny: what's the problem

Kick-Ass: i'm weak, cant really see myself do it

Claes: if i cared about u i'd kill myself just to show your sorry ass how tis done

Björn&Benny: u really r an arsehole, i bet one day u gonna go berserk in the school, kill us all, arsehole, go kill yrself instead

Claes: fuck u abba-lover

Administrator: That's it boys. You're out.

Chanel Nr 5: Kick-Ass, I've been following your conversation with the others. Are you seriously considering suicide?

Kick-Ass: i don't know, yes, i guess i do, what's it to u

Chanel Nr 5: But why? Are you in trouble in some way?

Kick-Ass: not really, it's just, don't know, what's the point, everything sucks

Chanel Nr 5: I must say I know what you mean. I had a

friend who was just about doing it. He went to the school psychiatrist and she really helped him back on his feet. Maybe you can give her a shot. Check out what she's got to offer. You have nothing to lose, right?

KICK-ASS: don't know, maybe, i'll see about that

CHANEL NR 5: You do that. I'm sure you'll get something out of it. You just seem such a nice guy. Just like that comic book character. Remember what he did. He fought against all odds, and he did kick some serious ass.

KICK-ASS: he was pretty cool

CHANEL NR 5: I'm a girl so I identify more with the little girl, but yes, he's very cool. I'm sure you are too.

KICK-ASS: yeah, whatever

CHANEL NR 5: Btw, my name's Almasa.

KICK-ASS: a'right, thanks for the chat, talk 2 u later, must dash to class now

CHANEL NR 5: You're right, me too, I'm late. Later then.

v

Oct 3, 2010. Chat-room 1. Users present: Björn&Benny, Jenny, Chanel Nr 5, Fiona

FIONA: nice to c u around jenny, we heard u killed yourself

JENNY: i thought i did, listened to some arsehole on the chat, but I cut my wrists the wrong way

BJÖRN&BENNY: amateur hour

FIONA: get out BB, u r not welcome here

BJÖRN&BENNY: sorry girls, just kidding, jenny I'm glad u r still alive n kicking

JENNY: not thanx 2 u, or that prick claes, someone called the nurse and she called my mum and i went 2 see this old woman, shrink, very nice one

FIONA: but u still did it

JENNY: yes, i guess the call was a little late, but my mum was desprat and hysteric she couldnt help me herself, so the nurse was welcome, an early Christmas gift i guess

CHANEL NR 5: Glad to hear you got help Jenny. Not everyone was that fortunate.

JENNY: what d u mean

CHANEL NR 5: There was a boy on the chat last month. Called himself Kick-Ass. Turned out no one knew who he was until two days ago. He was in the media programme. Made short films with his friends.

BJÖRN&BENNY: cut the chase will ya, what happened

CHANEL NR 5: Threw himself under a train, Pendeltåg station down in Älvsjö. His name was Stig.

FIONA: U must be joking. Stig, long brown hair, big arse.

CHANEL NR 5: Yes.

JENNY: don't know what 2 say

BJÖRN&BENNY: he really did kick ass, his own

JENNY: BB stop it. can someone up there kick BB outta here

ADMINISTRATOR: Done.

CHANEL NR 5: The worst thing is, I talked to him a few weeks ago and he said he was not feeling well. I told him to go to Linda but he never did.

FIONA: that's awful, he was a nice bloke

CHANEL NR 5: I think we should be more alert to these things. Help each other out. Support each other.

JENNY: I got support all right, but the other way round

FIONA: if this happens on the high school chat, what's going on on those nasty suicide chats

JENNY: i must say i never tried those

FIONA: maybe if u did u be dead now,

CHANEL NR 5: Glad to hear you are staying away from that sort of forum. I must go now, but I'm glad to hear you are all right Jenny. Take care.

JENNY: bye

FIONA: cheers

vi

Dec 25, 2010. Chat-room 7. Users present: Top-Notch, Uzi,

Cleopatra, Dan-Brown

UZI: can't fucking take it any more
DAN-BROWN: what up
UZI: I'm gonna end this shit
Top-Notch: u serious
UZI: fucking yeah
CLEOPATRA: u gonna use uzi Uzi
UZI: where the fuck can i get that kinda stuff, I'm just gonna throw myself under a tram, I heard it worked for this guy at Södra Latin high school . . .
DAN-BROWN: tram's weak ass shit, itll only bruise u
CHANEL NR 5: Uzi, u wanna meet and fuck?

AFTERWORD: HOMECOMING

A STRANGER has come
To share my room in the house not right in the head
— Dylan Thomas, 'Love in the Asylum'

i. Bouts of Nostalgia and Strangeness

In the spring of 2004, eleven years after coming to Sweden, I, the son of a factory worker, who had been ready to walk in my father's shoes, or maybe even become an engineer, because I was good with things and numbers, or so the men in my family let me believe, received a scholarship to write a Ph.D in English Literature, and for some reason I felt it was about time to venture on a sightseeing tour of my motherland, Bosnia and Herzegovina, or just plain Bosnia, as we Northerners say because we tend to discriminate against the Southerners with their weird accents and too-local vocabulary. (ps: Friends from the South, you know who you are, I'm just kidding.)

A year earlier, my house in Banja Luka had been emptied of its Serbian occupants, all according to the international agreements for the return of refugees, so I drove 2,500 km one-way through Europe, and it took me seven hours to cover one third of Sweden from Stockholm to Malmö, then over the miles-long bridge to the no-longer-rotten Denmark, a few hours of vomiting on the ferry, then racing on Germany's Autobahn without getting speeding tickets and seeing no thing German except for petrol stations and long car queues, and then I navigated through Austria's heavy mountain shadows, which cut deep into Slovenia as well.

Before the journey, I was warned about many things: the bad Balkan roads, the madness of (other) peoples' driving habits, where to drive slower to avoid fines, where to say what, and to whom, and how much it was reasonable to pay to pass along as smoothly as possible.

A trip like that, for the first time and with two kids in the backseat, was scary, especially when different people tell you different things. Bosnian passports had kept changing every couple of years and were still rumoured to cause longer stops, whereas the Swedish ones you could just wave at border crossings. I applied for one. I was prepared.

The Bosnian word zahod, which means toilet, appeared on huge Slovenian road signs, but in Slovenian it meant West and I thought of my uncle who would have know that, because he'd travelled the Balkans East-West-North-South and any other imaginary direction. I wound my way at snail-speed up and down narrow Balkan roads, just inches from grassy precipices, and with dozens of angry Croatian drivers trying to overtake me. Then I entered Bosnia at a border I'd never seen before, and a hundred more towns and villages whose names I vaguely recalled from geography lectures, before coming to the small familiar place called motherland, my city Banja Luka, my suburb Vrbanja.

My yard was overgrown with chamomile. The evening was hot and it was like floating inside the fumes of freshly brewed tea. I was more like Alice moving in the smoke from the caterpillar's hookah. Everything felt as real as a good steady dream, a dream that does not leave me when I wake. The next day, I walked around the neighbourhood. Unrecognizable faces moved like bodiless masks around familiar houses. Some of the homes were completely empty, as mine would be once I went back (home) to Sweden. It was nice and ghostly to be there again.

One thing struck me more than anything else. I knew I was supposed to register with the police because I was using a foreign passport, but it was such a ridiculous rule, and I was too overwhelmed when I saw my ex-home, I couldn't care less about post-war bureaucracy. I met some of my old neighbours who had returned. They scolded me for not returning to my roots for good. All that talk made me numb. I could not even think of how my two small boys were stomaching everything. All I knew was they were not causing much trouble.

Just before returning to Sweden, I was warned again to register myself in Bosnia and also to make sure that I unregistered. I went to the police and the sulky clerk asked me why I had not done it earlier. I shrugged my shoulders and told him I did not know I was supposed to. He retorted, You who live abroad just stream back in this country every damn summer. You feel you're coming back home and that everything is just hunky-dory. But you don't get that you're foreigners now. You're strangers here.

Right there and then, my home was, if anything, my strangeness.

ii. Mother Tongue

One other thing made me realize how estranged I was from Bosnia. The language. I hadn't forgotten it. On the contrary, I was something of a nativist struggling to preserve this rich heritage of words that even Goethe himself learnt so as to enjoy Bosnian poetry. Well, it was not poetry I had forgotten about, it was the excessive Bosnian swearing. Bosnians sometimes pride themselves on the flexibility of their language. All words can be used for invective. We even have special suffixes that make this possible.

This is what happened. My mum-in-law wanted to buy a whole grilled lamb for her nephew's wedding in another town. The groom and I went to get one from this man who had a BBQ place. While the toothless man served us chilled Fanta Mango out on the terrace and boasted about his business, inside the room with a big window and a grill in which six lambs were rolling, his skinny wife was chopping the seventh lamb to pieces and throwing me a smile whenever she caught me gawking at her huge, hatchet-shaped knife, which she would whet every few slices.

The man swore like mad, but he was not angry or unpleasant. He was cheerful. I had forgotten about Bosnian casual-language-strategy. In order to make his language less posh, to make it as casual and relaxed as possible, he stuffed his sentences with all variations of fuck, while his wife stuffed bags with chopped lamb. The topic was breakfast. It took the man five minutes to say: I woke up early this morning and went to the baker, Midhat. I bought three buns and a cup of ayran (sour milk), and I sat in the grass to enjoy my breakfast. What he really said was, So I fucking woke up, a motherfucking hour before the cocksucking rooster. And I felt, fuck its mother in the arse, what can I fucking do now? Fuck it. So I washed my bloody face, and waddled down the sister-fucking road to that cocksucker Midhat, who makes cunt-smelly buns, and I fucking bought three, fuck his mum in the . . . and I sat in the grass to fucking rest, and enjoy the cocksucking breakfast, before I had to go to the motherfucking hell-job.

Something like that. You get the gist.

I felt like a language Puritan. I had stopped using even the regular Fuck it, let alone this syntax: only-every-second-word-normal. I was a stranger again, a posh Swede (Swedish being famous for having few and quite innocuous invectives). Yet, not even Swedes are so posh. When they ask me to teach them a few words from my mother tongue, they always ask for invectives. Shakespeare's Caliban said he was thankful to Miranda for she taught him how to curse and he could curse

Prospero for his misfortune. This made me wonder, How in the world does a man forget to curse?

Now, back in the safe corridors of the English Department in Stockholm, a linguist colleague tells me that babies are exposed to their mother tongues even in the womb. It is an uncanny thing: swimming in a language like in the amniotic fluid, then swimming out of it as if I have emerged from the ice-cold Scandinavian sea on to some unfamiliar shore, breathless, and quite speechless. Quite curse-less.

ACKNOWLEDGEMENTS

The stories in this collection appeared in various journals and anthologies. 'Integration under the Midnight Sun' was first published by *The Rose and Thorn Journal* (and was The Pushcart Prize Nominee in 2006). 'Homecoming' too appeared in *The Rose and Thorn Journal*, 'Myth of the Smell' and 'Bayern, Bayern' in *Cantaraville*, and 'The Lovers' Discourse' in *Bevilderbliss*, and '[Refuge]e' in Ronin Press. 'First Day of Night' was published by *Stand Magazine* (2010) and won second place in Biscuit Publishing competition and appeared in the anthology *We're Créme de la Crem* (2011). 'Gusul' was originally a screenplay, which was filmed and released by Artwerk in 2010, and it was shortlisted in Willesden Herald 2011 competition judged by Maggie Gee. It was also included in an anthology *Stockholm Syndromes*. 'Vacation' was shortlisted in a *Glimmertrain* competition (2009) and commended by *The New Yorker*. It was published together with 'What We Talk About When We Talk About Suicide' in *Kerouac's Dog* (2011). 'Mind's Garbage' appeared in *The Battered Suitcase* and was performed at a conference on Jacques Derrida in Växsjö (2008), and at a conference on English as Lingua Franca in Brussels (2010).